Dear Reader,

I can hardly [believe that it is twenty years]
since I wrote my first Harlequin book. The thrill
of having that book accepted and then seeing it on
the bookshelves—being picked up and chosen by
readers—is one I shall never forget.

Twenty years seems a long time. So much has
happened during those years; so much has changed
and yet so much remains the same. The changes that
we have all seen within society are, I believe, reflected
in the books we, as Harlequin authors, write. They
mirror the changes that take place around us in
our own and our readers' lives. Our heroines have
changed, matured, grown up, as indeed I have done
myself. I cannot tell you how much pleasure it gives
me to be able to write of mature—as well as young—
women finding love. And, of course, love is something
that has not changed. Love is still love and always
will be, because love is, after all, an intrinsic, vital
component of human happiness.

As I read through these books that are being reissued
in this Collector's Edition, they bring back for me
many happy memories of the times when I wrote
them, and I hope that my readers, too, will enjoy
the same nostalgia and pleasure.

I wish you all very many hours of happy reading and
lives blessed with love.

Penny Jordan

Back by Popular Demand

Penny Jordan is one of the world's best loved as well as bestselling authors, and she was first published by Harlequin in 1981. The novel that launched her career was *Falcon's Prey*, and since then she has gone on to write more than one hundred books. In this special collection, Harlequin is proud to bring back a selection of these highly sought after novels. With beautiful cover art created by artist Erica Just, this is a Collector's Edition to cherish.

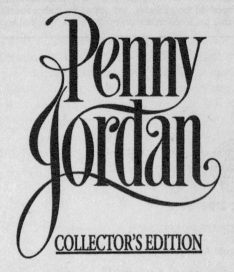

Penny Jordan

COLLECTOR'S EDITION

Passionate Possession

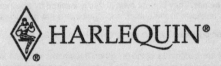

HARLEQUIN®

TORONTO • NEW YORK • LONDON
AMSTERDAM • PARIS • SYDNEY • HAMBURG
STOCKHOLM • ATHENS • TOKYO • MILAN • MADRID
PRAGUE • WARSAW • BUDAPEST • AUCKLAND

ISBN 0-373-63068-9

PASSIONATE POSSESSION

First North American Publication 1995.

ERICA JUST
cover illustrator for the
Penny Jordan Collector's Edition

Erica Just is an artist and illustrator working in various media, including watercolor, pen and ink, and textiles. Her studio is in Nottingham, England.

Her work is inspired by the natural forms, architecture and vibrant colors that she has experienced on her travels, most especially in Africa and India.

Erica has exhibited her work extensively in Great Britain and Europe and has works in private and public collections. As an illustrator she works for a number of companies and also lectures on textile design throughout the country.

CHAPTER ONE

'OF COURSE I haven't met him yet, but, from what
Don has been telling me about him, he's going to
prove a marvellous asset to us locally. I mean, all
that money, for one thing. It's a pity he's involved
with someone, though. Not that they're married, but
they *are* living together, at least they will be once
she comes back from New York. Apparently she's
over there on some kind of secondment. I'm ar-
ranging a small dinner party...just eight or ten of
us, to introduce him into the local community, and
of course we'll want you to be there. Lucy, are you
listening to me?'

Lucy forced herself to smile.

'Yes, of course I am, Verity. You were telling
me about Don's new client.'

'Yes, I was, but I don't think you were listening
properly,' Verity complained. 'I suppose you're still
worrying about that stupid old man. Honestly,
Lucy, why don't you simply sell the place and—?'

'I can't sell it because he's a sitting tenant,' Lucy

interrupted her patiently, 'and I haven't got the money to do the repairs that are needed.'

'He must *know* that. I'll bet that's why he's complaining.'

'He's complaining,' Lucy corrected her gently, 'because he has every right to do so. The house is in a bad state of repair, but I can't use it as security to borrow money against to have it seen to and I don't have any other way of raising any money. Unless I sell my flat.'

'But you can't do that,' Verity protested. 'Where on earth would you live?'

Lucy shook her head. Verity was kind-hearted enough, but she was also a rather self-centred and slightly spoiled woman who had never had to confront any major kind of financial problem in her whole life.

Lucy knew she did not really understand her own position, and if it had not been for the fact that Don, her husband, was Lucy's boss, coupled with the other fact that in her grandparents' time Lucy's family had been rather well-to-do and very well known in the neighbourhood, Lucy doubted that she would have been accepted socially by Verity.

Now both Lucy's grandparents and her parents were dead, and all that was left of the assets her family had once owned locally was the small, very run-down cottage property which Lucy had recently inherited from a several-times-removed cousin.

Lucy had been appalled when she had first heard the news from her cousin's solicitor. She knew the cottage, of course, but she had assumed that her cousin had sold it long ago to its long-time tenant. The news that she had not done so, and that she, Lucy, was now its owner and responsible for its appalling state of repair, had stunned her.

She had tentatively suggested that old Mr Barnes might wish to consider buying the cottage, but the letter she had received direct from him had made it plain that he had no intentions of doing any such thing...of wasting *his* money on repairing the cottage when it was *her* responsibility to do so.

Lucy had taken what advice she could, and as far as she could see there was no way out of the situation. She was undisputedly the owner of the cottage.

If she had been the type to give way to tears she would have given way to them then. She had struggled so hard to repair her life since the dreadful accident in which her parents had lost their lives. She had been seventeen then, with her whole future ahead of her. Her parents weren't wealthy, but with careful management they had decided that it would be possible for them to send Lucy to university.

With their death that had become impossible. Her

father had been a lovable and loving man, but a rather impractical one. He had not been properly insured; the house had had a large mortgage, and Lucy had quickly come to realise that her tiny inheritance was nowhere near enough to support her through university.

At first she had been too shocked, too filled with grief to think of the future...of her future, but, kind though everyone was, there had eventually come a time when Lucy had realised that she could not go on living with the family friends who had taken her in; that the pitifully small amount in what was now her sole bank account was not going to last forever and that it was time for her to make plans for her future.

She had taken a secretarial course, one that concentrated on the basic secretarial skills and computer familiarisation. It had been an expensive intensive course, but very worthwhile, giving her a thorough grounding in those basics. To them she added the languages she had learned at school and then polished at night school, so that she was proficient in both German and French.

Initially she had planned to look for work in London, but, excellent though the salaries had seemed, she had soon realised that with the very high cost of living she would barely be able to manage, and so instead she had taken a junior typist's job locally, and, taking her solicitor's advice, she had used her small inheritance to buy a tiny one-bedroom flat in a conversion development being built on the outskirts of the town in what had once been a large Victorian house.

That, she now acknowledged, had been one of the best pieces of advice anyone could have given her.

There was certainly no way now she could ever have afforded to buy even such a modest property of her own at present-day costs. Don paid her well, she lived comfortably, ran a small compact car, took her annual holidays abroad, entertained her friends, and even occasionally splurged on good clothes, but there was no way she could find the many thousands of pounds required to repair Cousin Emily's run-down cottage.

Her only savings were the small insurance pension she had started on her twenty-first birthday, and the few hundred pounds she had in her building-society account.

Lucy did not consider herself poor nor hard done by; after all, she had a good and very pleasant job, working for a man she liked and who made it plain that he valued her professional skills. She had good friends, enough money to get by on, and she had her health. She also had her pride, something she had discovered in those awful months after her parents' death, when she had abruptly come to hear herself being described as 'that poor child', and had realised sensitively that people felt sorry for her; that in some way they blamed her parents for not making better provision for her. There had even been whispered conversations about how dreadful it was that a family which had been so prominent locally and been so wealthy should have fallen so far, almost as though her poor parents had been responsible for the disappearance of that wealth, which Lucy knew was not the case at all.

She had longed to defend her parents, to tell their friends that neither her father nor her mother had considered money to be of prime importance, but at seventeen they were still treating her like a child.

She had resolved then to find a way of standing on her own two feet, and now her independence, as well as being something she privately cherished, was so much a part of her that occasionally the braver of her friends would tease her a little about it.

Perhaps she was a little over-independent, over-determined to prove she could manage, but her friends had never been in her situation, had never discovered almost overnight that they were no longer a loved and protected only child with caring parents, but completely alone in the world with only themselves to rely on.

If anyone had asked her Lucy would have answered quickly, and she believed honestly, that at twenty-six she was completely over the trauma of losing her parents, and of the consequent discovery of her vulnerability emotionally and financially, but the shock of discovering all the problems attached to her unexpected and unwanted inheritance had shaken that belief. She felt vulnerable and afraid again, so much so that she had broken one of her unwritten rules and had confided her dilemma to Don.

As an accountant, he had warned her of the problems she was likely to face in view of the property's run-down state and its sitting tenant; as a friend, he had consoled her as best he could, and unfortunately, as a husband, he had discussed the situation with Verity.

Not that Lucy had expected him not to. Verity, after all, was a good friend, but she was a terrible gossip, and Lucy suspected that there could be very few people who did not know about her problems with the cottage now, thanks to Verity.

The trouble with Verity was that she did not have enough to occupy her time or her mind. Their two sons were away at public school, and Verity spent most of her time either shopping or gossiping. She also had a tendency to embroider the facts, and Lucy tensed now as she heard Verity exclaiming sympathetically and indignantly, 'It's all Eric Barnes's fault...trying to make all this trouble for you...he's been living in that cottage for years. He should have complained to your cousin.'

'He did,' Lucy told her patiently. 'But Emily was virtually senile. I doubt she even read his letters, never mind understood them. I used to go and visit her, you know. The people in the home were very kind, but she barely recognised them, let alone me.'

'But there must be something you can do,' Verity consoled.

'Yes. There is. Sell my flat,' Lucy repeated grimly. She got up, putting her fragile china teacup down.

Don was away on business, and she had called round with some papers she had been translating for him. Don had several clients who were investing in properties in France, and it fell to Lucy to translate the correspondence received from France concerning these properties.

'Oh, you don't have to go yet, do you?' Verity complained. 'I haven't finished telling you about Niall Cameron. You'd never guess he was Scotch.'

'A Scot,' Lucy corrected her automatically. 'Scotch is a drink.'

'Scotch...Scottish...what does it matter?' Verity demanded slightly petulantly, adding quickly, 'Anyway, as I was telling you, he's incredibly wealthy. Apparently he's built up this huge business to do with computers, and he's opening a factory not far away on that new industrial park just outside Tetfield. He's bought Hawkins Farm as well—'

'Yes, Verity, I do know,' Lucy interrupted her, adding wryly, 'I work for Don, remember.'

'Yes, but you were away when it happened. You haven't even met him yet.'

'No,' Lucy agreed.

She didn't particularly want to meet Niall Cameron either, she decided with distaste. He sounded the type of man she most disliked. Arrogant...full of his own importance, forever boasting about his achievements.

She was glad she had been away when he had moved to the area, although it seemed that she wasn't going to be allowed to put off meeting him much longer, not if Verity had her way and organised this dinner party.

'I wish Don would buy *us* a property in France,' Verity was saying poutingly now. 'All our friends are doing it. I mean, you pick up the most marvellous things over there for next to nothing. The Martindales have bought the most fabulous château...with fifteen bedrooms.'

'And no bathrooms nor any running water,' Lucy told her wryly.

She knew. She had been over in France for the last month, working for Don, acting as both his representative and a translator for those of his clients who were involved in buying French properties.

It had been a hectic six weeks, demanding and challenging; she had enjoyed the work, although sometimes she had found the attitude of Don's clients hard to understand. Many of them seemed to have no conception at all of what the purchase of their French properties was going to involve.

In many cases the properties themselves were virtually derelict, and yet the new owners were talking happily of summers spent lavishly entertaining the friends they expected to come hurrying over from England to admire and envy their newest acquisitions.

It was true that there were some who genuinely seemed to know what they were getting themselves into and who seemed to be prepared to make all the adjustments they would need to make to be able to live in such rural communities. For the most part, though... She sighed a little to herself, remembering the look on the face of one woman when she had discovered that her fourteenth-century farmhouse had neither any sanitation nor any electricity, and that when it rained the lane to it became a marshy bog through which their immaculate Daimler saloon could not possibly travel.

'I must go,' she told Verity.

'Oh-ho…got a date tonight?' Verity asked archly.

Lucy forced herself to smile.

'Tom's taking me to the theatre,' she told her.

'Tom Peters. He's divorced now, isn't he?'

'Yes,' Lucy agreed quietly.

She and Tom were old friends, and she knew how much he had suffered during the break-up of his marriage. She liked him and felt sorry for him, but friends were all they were.

Lucy was as cautious with her emotions as she was with everything else.

She was afraid to fall in love, one of her boyfriends had once accused her. Perhaps it was true. Perhaps the loss of her parents, coming when it had, had somehow instilled in her an inability to take the kind of emotional risks that went with loving someone. Or perhaps it was her own nature she feared; the knowledge that beneath her calm surface ran very deep and intense emotions and passions.

As she walked towards the door she gave a small shrug. She was twenty-six years old and she enjoyed being single; what was wrong with that? She wasn't the kind of woman who needed to have a sexual relationship in her life; she preferred men's friendship to their sexual advances, and was always very firm about making that quite plain.

She had had one or two problems at first in France in that regard, but a cool smile and the information that she never, ever mixed business with pleasure had soon solved them.

Her car was parked next to Verity's Mercedes coupé.

'What on earth made you choose a car that colour?' Verity demanded as she came out to see her off and frowned over the plain grey body of Lucy's small Ford.

'I liked it,' Lucy told her. 'It's discreet and practical.'

She smiled as she spoke, knowing that Verity would not understand. Verity was a creature of colour, an extrovert who demanded to be noticed. Lucy was not like that.

She liked to blend into her background, not stand out from it. She smiled a little over the difference in their appearances. Verity was wearing a scarlet suit, and her make-up was equally vivid. She, Lucy, was wearing a cream silk shirt worn outside a camel-coloured straight skirt. Her toffee-brown hair was cut neatly to her shoulders, its straightness enhancing its healthy shine. Her make-up was minimal and discreet; her pale matt skin needed no foundation, just a hint of blusher along her cheekbones to bring them warmth, a touch of grey shadow around her eyes to emphasise the elegance of their almond shape. That they were a particularly vivid shade of turquoise blue was something that had always made Lucy feel slightly uncomfortable; hazel or, better still, grey eyes would have been far more in keeping with the image she chose to project. Turquoise was somehow far too theatrical, far too noticeable.

Her lipstick was a discreet peachy pink. She wore the minimum she could get away with because her mouth was, in her eyes, a little too large, her lips rather too full.

'Why is it that *you* always manage to look sexy without even trying?' one of her friends had once complained.

Lucy had been horrified by her question and still sometimes rather anxiously searched her reflection in the mirror, looking uncomfortably for this supposed sexiness, which thankfully was not apparent to her.

She got into her car and started the engine, a serene-looking woman who rarely allowed others close enough to her to guess what that outward serenity sometimes cost her.

Her flat was on the opposite side of their small local town to where Don and Verity lived, but, instead of taking the more direct route through the town itself, Lucy turned the car towards the open countryside.

The cottage she had inherited from her cousin was well outside the town, all that was left of the several good-sized farms and their lands that had once been owned by her family. The big house, the house built by her great-great-grandfather, had been demolished shortly after the war, but, from what she had seen of it from photographs, there was no reason to regret its destruction. It had been a rather ugly and over-large building which her father remembered as being extremely cold and uncomfortable.

The cottage must have originally been a part of one of the farms and had probably been built to house a farm labourer and his family.

It had a good-sized garden, now completely overgrown and something of an eyesore.

That had been another of Eric Barnes's complaints. Her cousin, as his landlord, should have done something about the garden, he had told her when Lucy had visited him in an attempt to try and explain to him her situation.

It had not been a pleasant meeting. Eric Barnes was, in Lucy's opinion, a misogynist. He had been aggressive and unpleasant towards her, making all sorts of impossible financial demands, but against her immediate dislike of him was the fact that the cottage was in a disgraceful condition.

The roof leaked, and one bedroom was virtually

uninhabitable because of this. The house had no proper heating; just an ancient stove in the kitchen and open fires in the other rooms. The bathroom had horrified Lucy as she had surveyed the fungus- and mould-tainted walls and the cracked, grimy tiles. And as for the kitchen... She suspected it was probably a health hazard, but this was as much Eric Barnes's fault as the cottage's.

He had seen the swift look of distaste she had not quite been quick enough to hide when she had seen the greasy grey water in the washing-up bowl, the remains of food on a table which had looked as though it hadn't been cleaned in weeks, and he had immediately jeered at her, taunting her, making to- tally invalid comments about her supposed wealth and her family's position, even threatening to reveal her negligence to the local Press.

Lucy had been taken aback by his vindictiveness. She had come fully prepared to apologise for the state of the cottage and to explain to him her own position, but his attitude had made this impossible.

Since then she had learned that he had the rep- utation of being a very difficult old man, who ap- parently conducted a series of running battles with all the local care agencies, alternately demanding their services and then rejecting them with a barrage of unfair complaints.

'He just likes causing trouble; he's that kind of

man,' someone had feelingly told Lucy, but none
of that altered the fact that the cottage was not really fit to live in, nor that it was her responsibility.

Her solicitor had gently pointed out to her her
obligations as a landlord, adding that, because of
her cousin's mental health, it would have been impossible for any real case to have been brought
against *her*, but that Lucy was not similarly protected.

'But what can I do?' she had asked helplessly.

Her solicitor had shaken his head. They both
knew there was nothing she could do. Not unless
she sold her own home.

Lucy slowed down as she approached the cottage. It was set back from the main road in its tan-
gled, untidy garden, surrounded by green fields. It
should have looked a pleasant spot, but instead…

Lucy sighed as she surveyed it. Upstairs a window yawned emptily where apparently the distorted
frame had fallen out in the winter storms. The black
polythene which had been used to cover it did not
present an attractive sight. The remainder of the
window-frames were warped, what paint there was
left on them blistered and flaking off. Grimy net
curtains covered the downstairs windows. There
was an ominous bulge in the wall at the side of the
cottage where apparently there were some serious
structural defects, and on the other side a lean-to of

sorts had been constructed with a corrugated-iron roof, which was now rusting and even holed in places.

It was in there that Eric Barnes stored the coal for his fires, and he had complained to Lucy that the holes in the roof were making the coal almost too damp to use.

In the garden, overgrown shrubs and brambles almost but not quite concealed several rusting piles of rubbish, items which Eric Barnes claimed had been in the house when he had taken up occupation. The wooden gate fronting the lane was hanging off its hinges and rotting.

Her heart heavy, Lucy drove on. Even without its unpleasant tenant it would have been difficult to sell the cottage. *Sell it*! It would have been difficult to *give* it away in its present state, she admitted.

Her hands clenched on the steering-wheel. She tried to force herself to relax. She was fine-boned and slim, but recently friends had begun to comment that she was looking a little too drawn, a little too fragile.

That was the cost of her outward serenity, the fact that inwardly she worried and that that worrying cost her weight she could not afford to lose.

It was almost six o'clock and she realised that her detour had meant that she was going to have to rush to be ready when Tom came to pick her up.

She decided to take a short cut through the new business park.

The mayor had opened it less than a year ago, and she had to admit that it was well designed and laid out, or at least it would be once the newly planted trees started to mature.

Now, on a Saturday afternoon, it was relatively quiet. Most of the units were quite small; this was not a big industrial area, after all, and none of them was above three storeys in height.

One of the largest units was the complex taken up by Niall Cameron for his software company.

She had been a little surprised when Don had first told her about Niall Cameron. 'Why on earth is he relocating down here?' she had asked him.

'Personal reasons,' Don had told her. She presumed now, after listening to Verity, that those personal reasons must in some way concern the woman with whom he was living. Perhaps, since she was presently working in New York, her work took her abroad a good deal and they were reasonably close to the airport here, and Manchester Airport was expanding rapidly to provide most international flights.

Without being aware of what she was doing, she had slowed down slightly as she had approached the Cameron complex. A brand-new Discovery was

parked outside it. Lucy grimaced to herself as she
surveyed its gleaming paintwork.

It wouldn't stay like that for very long if he actually moved into the farm. The lane to the farm
was rutted and invariably muddy whenever they
had any rain.

She stiffened as she saw a man emerge from the
building and walk towards the Discovery. He was
tall, bare-headed and in his mid-thirties, his dark
hair lifting in the breeze. Those immaculately polished shoes wouldn't last very long in that state
either, she decided sardonically as she watched him.
He was dressed in city-smart 'casual' clothes—a
leather blouson jacket, immaculately pressed trou-
sers, a fine-checked wool shirt—all very smart and
all very expensive. Her top lip curled a little.

The right clothes, the right accent... Oh, yes, she
could see why Verity was so impressed by him. He
had stopped moving and he was, she realised with
a small stab of disquiet, watching her. There was
no reason why she should not be where she was,
but for some reason she immediately panicked, putting the car into gear and almost stalling it as she
did so, her face suddenly hot and flushed, her breath
coming far too quickly.

She didn't like him, she decided as she drove
jerkily away.

She did not like him one tiny, little bit.

CHAPTER TWO

LATER on that evening as she sat beside Tom, half-heartedly paying attention to the play being unfolded below them on the stage, Lucy allowed herself to admit that her judgement of Niall Cameron was perhaps illogical.

After all, he was not the only man to drive an expensive vehicle, to wear expensive clothes. Nor had she any reason to dislike him simply because he had moved to the area. Was it perhaps Verity's breathless admiration for him that had jarred against her? It certainly couldn't be his wealth; despite her own position, Lucy had no desire to be wealthy. Not to have to worry so much about money perhaps, but the luxuries money could buy...no, she had no envy of those.

So why, then? Why had the man aroused such antagonism in her, both before and after she had seen him?

'Not still worrying about the cottage, are you?' Tom asked her during the interval.

'Not really,' Lucy fibbed. 'Why?'

'You just seem rather preoccupied, that's all.'

'It's nothing,' Lucy assured him, asking, 'Isn't it your Sunday for the children tomorrow?'

'Yes.' Tom frowned. 'Josy claims that seeing me upsets them too much. God, hasn't she made me feel guilty enough already? It was her decision to go for a divorce, not mine.'

Lucy said nothing. She had heard the gossip about the brief illicit affair which had been the fore-runner to Tom's divorce. He was nice enough, but inclined to be rather self-indulgent and a little weak. At the moment he was too full of self-pity to be ready to admit that it was his own adultery which had led to Josy's decision to divorce him, although Lucy suspected that there had been other problems in the marriage. She was not the kind of person who liked prying into the private lives of her friends.

'God knows what I'm going to do with them. The kids, I mean. That damned flat is so small.'

Lucy watched him gravely. She suspected that Tom was already getting bored with playing the doting, misunderstood daddy. How long would it be before he found excuses for not seeing his children every week? How long would it be before he lost contact with them altogether? Lucy felt a small spurt of anger against him. His children loved him...needed him, and she did not doubt that he loved them, but she suspected that he loved himself more. She chastised herself for her thoughts. What right did she have to criticise? She had no children...no partner...she knew nothing of the stresses the break-up of a marriage could bring.

Even so, without intending to, she heard herself asking quietly, 'Is it really too late, Tom, for you and Josy?'

They had been so very much in love when they had married, Tom twenty-six, the same age as she was now, Josy just twenty. Now, five years later, they were divorced, claiming that they no longer loved one another. But they had two small children, whom they both did love. What was wrong with society, Lucy wondered bleakly, that there should be so much confusion and suffering? She remembered clearly the love she had received from her parents, from both of them, and how she had felt when she had lost that love, and she had almost been adult.

'You don't approve, do you?' Tom accused her suddenly, surprising her with his unexpected astuteness.

'It has nothing to do with me, Tom,' she told him mildly.

'No,' he agreed wryly. 'But you haven't answered my question, have you? You know what your trouble is, don't you, Lucy? You're out of touch with reality. You live in this rarefied world where everyone does the right thing, where everyone is perfect and behaves properly. My God, is it any wonder that you live there alone?' he added, savagely shocking her with the vehemence of his words. Words that hurt her, even though she didn't show it.

'Wonderful, wonderful Lucy,' he derided. 'You've never put a foot wrong, have you? You'll never make a mistake, will you...you'll never fall in love with a married man...break *your* marriage vows...? You'd never do anything that isn't perfectly correct, would you?'

Lucy fought not to show how much his anger had shocked her. Raw emotion of this kind frightened her, making her remember how she had felt when she had first learned of her parents' death. Since then she had learned to control her emotions, not to show them, and somehow being in the presence of someone who didn't share that kind of control made her feel nervous and vulnerable.

'I hope I would never do anything that might hurt someone else,' she told him gravely.

The look he gave her was bitter.

'You don't even begin to know what life's about, do you?' he challenged savagely. 'Do you think *I* wanted to have an affair? Do you think I *planned* it?'

He was, Lucy recognised, under enormous emotional strain. She sincerely pitied him, but there was nothing she could do to help him. He might not have planned to be unfaithful, but surely there had been a point when he had known what was going to happen…a stage at which he could have chosen to draw back?

'What happens if you fall in love with the wrong man, Lucy…a man who loves you in return but who's committed to someone else…or do you simply think that that would never happen?' he jeered.

Thankfully the bell for the second half rang before she needed to make any response, but Tom's words stayed with her, challenging her. She would never allow herself to fall in love with a man who was committed to someone else. It simply could not happen, she knew that, but somehow Tom's words, his anger, had unsettled her. He had made her sound so…so cold and emotionless, which she wasn't. Why should she be made to feel like that? To love a man who was hurting someone else, cheating on someone else, a someone else who had every right to his love and his loyalty, to be with her—no, she could never do that. To rob another woman of her lover, children of their father. She knew too well how it felt to suffer that kind of loss.

They were both very quiet as Tom drove her home. When he parked outside the block of flats he apologised abruptly, 'I'm sorry. It's just… Well, it's been one hell of a week. I wanted to see Josy…to talk to her, but she…' He shrugged, and in the darkness Lucy could see the pain in his eyes. 'I'm afraid I just took my frustration out on you.'

'What else are friends for?' Lucy asked him lightly.

He made no attempt to touch or kiss her, but then she had not expected that he would. They did not have that kind of relationship. Lucy had never encouraged her male friends and acquaintances to be physically affectionate towards her.

Even with her first lover she had remained slightly aloof and distant in public.

She smiled a little as she let herself into her flat.

She had been almost twenty-one when she had rather gravely decided that she could hardly remain a virgin forever. She and Harris had worked together. He had been five years her senior, a rather studious and quiet biochemist. They had got on well together and she had persuaded herself that she was in love with him. They had planned to get engaged, but almost immediately that they became lovers Lucy had realised that what she had mistaken for love was in actual fact merely affection and liking.

He had been a considerate lover, careful and gentle, but she had certainly not experienced with him anything intense enough to make her feel the way she knew other people felt about their men.

They had parted amicably and as friends. He had moved away from the area now and they had not remained in contact. She had no regrets about knowing him and even less about not marrying him.

Was Tom right? Was she over-controlled? She looked at her reflection gravely as she cleaned off her make-up. What was she supposed to do? Give in to every tiny emotion she felt, abandon herself to them, embellish and exaggerate them? No. That was not her way.

She told herself that she was being silly, that Tom had not meant to be deliberately hurtful, but somehow that made it worse.

Beyond her bedroom window was the familiar outline of the trees ringing the grounds surrounding the flats. The developer had been forced to keep those trees; she was lucky, living here. Maybe her neighbours were all elderly...maybe the flat was small, but at least it was hers. Her haven...her security.

She shivered a little. How much longer would she be able to keep it if Eric Barnes continued to press her to repair the cottage?

Beside her bed there was a photograph of her parents.

Her father had always wanted to be a painter. It was the one disappointment of his life that he was, as he had put it, good enough to know he was just not good enough. Lucy knew that sometimes it had frustrated him that he could only have as a hobby something he would have liked to have made his whole life.

The trip to Provence had been a special treat her parents had given themselves. A twenty-fifth wedding-anniversary present. Lucy wasn't able to go with them because they had to take advantage of a cheaper out-of-school-holiday-time offer.

It had been a hot, dry summer, and when first she had heard of the fires sweeping France she had had no intimation, no intuitive sense of what was to come.

Her parents hadn't been the only ones to lose their lives in those fires. There had been so many other deaths that perhaps it was understandable that the authorities had only been able to send that brusque telegram.

She had been alone when it had arrived, and at first she had not been able to take in what had happened.

She sat down on her bed, blinking rapidly, fiercely refusing to allow herself to cry. It was almost ten years ago now, but she still missed them…still missed their love.

She did not, as she knew some of his friends had, blame her father for not taking more financial precautions…for not at least insuring his life, so that there would be something for her. After all, how could he have known, any more than she had, what was to come? And her parents had given her one priceless, precious gift: they had given her love. The kind of love that Tom's two small children did not have.

Was that part of the reason why she knew she could never do as so many others did and allow herself to become involved with someone who had commitments elsewhere? Or was she, as Tom had implied, simply too cold and prudish to ever experience the intense, heady physical desire that drove everything else out, including honour and self-respect?

Tiredly she climbed into bed. Rather than philosophising over something that was never likely to happen, she ought to be directing her thoughts to more important things. Like what she was going to do about the cottage and about its tenant.

Perhaps if she tried again to reason with Eric Barnes, to explain her situation...

A DINNER PARTY was the very last thing she felt like tonight, Lucy acknowledged as she stood under the shower, but Verity would never forgive her if she didn't turn up. Her non-appearance would put out Verity's numbers.

Perhaps because she had very little else to occupy her time Verity was almost obsessional about such things.

To Lucy's knowledge, she had rung Don at least four times during the week to consult him about proposed changes in her planned menu.

Lucy had winced a little at the irritation she could hear in Don's voice on the final occasion, but she had tactfully said nothing, and now here she was, getting ready to play the role Verity had set for her.

'Of course, I'm partnering you with Niall Cameron,' Verity had told her. 'After all, you're both single.'

'Single? I thought you said he was living with someone,' Lucy had reminded her.

'Yes, he is, but you know what I mean. I meant that he'll be coming alone, and so will you.'

'I hope you aren't thinking of doing any matchmaking,' Lucy had told her drily.

'Certainly not,' Verity had assured her.

But she hadn't been able to resist asking, 'Have you met him yet? He really is—'

'I haven't met him, but I have seen him,' Lucy had interrupted her, guessing what she was going to say. 'He definitely isn't my type.'

Verity's eyes had rounded.

'Lucy, he's *every* woman's type,' she had told her fatuously.

'I don't like arrogant men,' Lucy had overruled

her, and for once Verity had seemed to have nothing to say.

No, it wasn't going to be a particularly congenial evening, but she was too fond of Verity to upset her by refusing her invitation, and Don had been a good and generous boss to her. And, after all, what would she have to do, other than be polite to the man...a man who was one of their clients?

She gave a tiny shrug and then grimaced as she realised that she had soaped the same leg twice.

Lucy was as careful in buying her clothes as she was about everything else. Her job was such that she was often required to mix socially with Don's clients, as indeed she was doing tonight and as she had done while in France, and, apart from her very casual clothes—the jeans she kept for the long country tramps she enjoyed, her tennis kit, her comfortable loose sweaters—most of her wardrobe was geared to her working life.

Tonight she was wearing a very simple dark blue crêpe wool dress with a round neckline and a dropped waist. The skirt was gently gathered on the dropped waistline and narrowed elegantly towards the hem. It had long sleeves and fastened up the back with pearl buttons.

It was Italian, like a good many of her clothes, because the Italians seemed to specialise in clothes for women of her height.

With it she wore sheer tights and plain navy
suede pumps. Her only jewellery was the things she
had inherited from her mother. Three strands of
good cultured pearls, her rings, a pair of pearl ear-
rings and a very heavy red-gold bracelet.

The neckline of her dress wasn't suitable for the
pearls, so she wore the bracelet. Not for anything
would she have ever admitted to anyone that she
wore these things not just as a memento, but as a
kind of safeguard…a security blanket for when she
was feeling vulnerable.

As she brushed her hair she paused, wondering
what she had to feel vulnerable about tonight. She
knew everyone who was going to be there, everyone except Niall Cameron, and even he wasn't a
complete stranger to her. She had seen him; she
knew a good deal about his business; she even
knew that he had purchased the farm in his own
name rather than in the joint names of himself and
his lover. She smiled cynically to herself. That
showed the kind of man he was, didn't it? Not a
man who believed in sharing, obviously.

She wondered briefly what the woman was like.
Confident of herself and him, evidently; certainly
confident enough to leave him for so many months
while she was in New York.

She amused herself by building a mental picture
of her. She would be tall and elegant, blonde, per-

haps, with patrician features. Certainly not a pouty
bimbo type. He would want a woman who could
match him in style and looks, a woman who dressed
as elegantly and expensively as he did himself; a
woman who would look equally as at home in the
sophisticated cities of the world as she would standing beside that immaculately polished Discovery,
her hair just slightly touched by the breeze, a couple
of gun dogs at her side…chocolate-brown ones, of
course. An unkind smile touched Lucy's mouth.
She was being bitchy and probably very unfair, she
told herself, but she just couldn't help it; there was
something about the man, something about the way
he had looked at her…virtually as though she had
been an interloper, which had grated on her.

Was that how she felt, secretly? Did she feel she
was an outsider…that she was alone? A tiny tremulous sensation fluttered inside her.

Of course not. Now she was being silly. She had
good friends…close friends…and, if she didn't get
a move on, one of those friends was going to be
extremely irritated with her, she reminded herself.

Verity hated people being late. Surprisingly, perhaps, she was an excellent cook, and if nothing else
Lucy knew that she would enjoy her dinner.

There were several other cars in the drive when
Lucy arrived, including the Discovery. It was, Lucy
was amused to note, not quite as immaculate as it

had been when she had first seen it. There were distinct signs of mud-splashes on its shiny paint-work, and in the light from the powerful security lights around the house she could see how that same mud was clinging to the vehicle's tyres.

She wondered mischievously if his highly polished shoes had suffered the same fate. From what she remembered, the farm's cobbled yard was every bit as dirty as the lane.

Once that farm had been owned by her family, and let to tenants, but that had been before she was born.

She realised when Don let her in that she was the last to arrive. The others were gathered in the drawing-room, exchanging chit-chat over their pre-dinner drinks.

Don, knowing that she didn't drink, immediately poured her a glass of mineral water.

She had seen Niall Cameron the moment she had walked into the room. He was standing by the fire-place and was deep in conversation with Bill Broughton, a local builder. His wife was also with them, gazing very attentively at Niall Cameron. Bill had been a widower for eight years when he had married Amanda. She was fifteen years younger than him, thirty-five to his fifty, which must have made her around the same age as Niall Cameron, Lucy guessed.

She didn't know why, because she certainly wasn't staring at them, but for some reason something must have alerted Niall Cameron to her observation, because he turned his head and then moved so that he had an unobstructed view of her.

Did he recognise her? *Had* he really seen her in her car, or was he simply trying to place her? Her heart was beating a little bit too fast. She was suddenly sharply conscious of the sounds all around her, people's voices, the chink of glasses, hypersensitively aware, hyper-conscious that Niall Cameron was watching her.

'I think I'll go and see if Verity wants a hand in the kitchen,' she told Don huskily.

She had seen Niall Cameron start to move. It was ridiculous to imagine that he was intending to seek her out…absurd for her to feel that she must escape, especially when she was going to be seated with him at dinner, but for once her physical reactions were outside her mental control.

'Verity has Mary to help her,' Don was telling her, obviously puzzled, but Lucy ignored him, heading for the kitchen, where she found Verity instructing Mary Lewis. Mary was a widow and lived alone. As she had once told Lucy, she enjoyed helping out at dinner parties and functions because it allowed her to add to her income without tying her

down too much. Lucy smiled at her as she entered
the kitchen.

Verity, as always, looked immaculate, her nails
lacquered, her silk dress free of any kind of crease.

'Mm...watercress soup,' Lucy enthused as she
saw their first course.

'Yes, and salmon to follow.' Verity made a face.
'Rather dull, really, but Don loves it. I don't think
I've got any veggies. I didn't check with Niall
Cameron, although he doesn't look...'

'No, definitely a blood-red-meat man,' Lucy
agreed sardonically.

Verity gave her a confused look. 'I thought you
hadn't met him yet.'

Lucy sighed. Much as she liked Verity, she had
to admit that they weren't always on the same
wavelength.

'Shall I help?' she offered, but Verity immediately shook her head.

'No, no. Everything's under control.' She turned
to Mary. 'You'll bring the soup through in five
minutes, won't you, Mary?' she checked as she
shooed Lucy out of the kitchen and then followed
her, saying, 'Where's Don? I want him to get everyone into the dining-room.'

As she took her seat Lucy was amused to note
the tiny silver apples holding name-place cards.
Trust Verity.

She was just about to sit down when she heard someone saying, 'Allow me.'

It had to be Niall Cameron, of course. She tensed as he pulled out the chair for her, and then turned to thank him.

He was taller close to than she had expected. Six feet plus. He was also extremely broad-shouldered, more so than she would have imagined, and, although his suit fitted him perfectly, she had an uneasy feeling that the body beneath it was somehow very primitive and male. It was an odd feeling for her to have. She didn't normally entertain any kind of thoughts about men's bodies, primitive or otherwise.

'I don't think we've met.'

His voice was deep, its tone measured and polite, but certainly not effusive. He was being courteous, but not making any kind of attempt to impress her.

'No, not yet…not officially,' she agreed. 'I'm Lucy Howard.'

'Yes.'

He didn't smile at her, and a tiny trickle of nervous awareness touched her skin. It seemed that her prejudices against him were matched, if not surpassed, by his against her. Certainly there was no warmth in his eyes when he looked at her. Rather the opposite. He was openly studying her, assessing her, and not in the way that she was used to being assessed by the male sex.

'I…I work for Don,' she added quickly, and then wondered why on earth she had felt it necessary to add that explanation…that apology almost.

'Yes,' he agreed again.

They were both sitting down now. Mary was serving the soup and, since the man seated on her left was busily engaged in conversation with the woman to his left, Lucy had no option but at least make some attempt to converse with Niall Cameron.

'You're a newcomer to the area,' she began.

'Yes,' he agreed. 'Unlike you. Your family are very well known locally. Large landowners.'

Lucy put down her spoon. Was she imagining it, or had that really been antagonism in his voice? And what an extraordinary thing for him to say. It was well over fifty years since her family had last owned land.

'Er—yes…once…' she began, but was interrupted as the man to her left turned towards her and began talking to her.

Verity, as always, had produced an excellent meal, but Lucy was conscious that she did not do it justice. She could not understand why Niall Cameron was having such an extraordinary effect on her or why he was making her feel so nervous...so anxious.

She knew that he didn't like her, but *she* didn't like him, and so that was no reason for the tiny darting sensation of panic she could feel building in her stomach, spoiling her enjoyment of her meal.

Everyone else was now pleasantly relaxed and mellow. Perhaps she should have drunk her wine after all, Lucy thought grimly. She certainly couldn't remember the last time she had felt as on edge as this. Normally she was quite comfortable socially. Even when she had gone to France on business, she had not experienced this degree of tension and anxiety.

Now, with the plates cleared away and the conversation general as people enjoyed their coffee, Verity called down the table to her.

'Have you managed to do anything about the cottage yet, Lucy?' And then before Lucy could reply she was explaining for Niall Cameron's benefit, 'Poor Lucy is in the most wretched situation. She recently inherited a property from a cousin, a pretty little cottage, really, and in the most glorious setting, but it's tenanted by this appalling old man.'

Verity always liked to embroider her stories, Lucy reflected wryly as she mentally compared Verity's almost lyrical description of the cottage with its reality.

'And he's behaving dreadfully, isn't he, Lucy? Demanding that she makes all sorts of alterations, threatening to take her to court. Of course, the rent he pays is next to nothing. He shouldn't be living there at all, really. He ought to be in a home. From what Lucy's seen, it's obvious that he isn't fit to live alone, and if he would only move out Lucy could—'

'Sell the cottage and its land to some speculative builder,' Niall Cameron interposed grimly.

Lucy stared at him, and even Verity looked a little perplexed. One or two of the others were listening now as well, obviously as aware as Lucy was herself of the dislike and the condemnation in Niall Cameron's voice.

'Oh, Lucy wouldn't do anything like that,' Verity told him, obviously shocked. 'She just wants to—'

'To what?' Niall demanded. 'To bully a frail old man of almost eighty into leaving his home so that she can sell it and make a nice profit?'

Verity was gaping at him now.

'Oh, but you don't understand,' she began helplessly. 'Eric Barnes is the most obnoxious man, and poor Lucy—'

'Oh, but I do understand,' Niall told her softly. 'You see, that obnoxious old man, as you call him, just happens to be my uncle.'

He turned to Lucy, who was staring at him in

shock, and told her grimly, 'I am beginning to see now *why* he is so afraid of you. I warn you, Miss Howard, there are laws to prevent people like you from defaming people, just as there are laws, very strong laws, to force landlords to fulfil their obligations towards their tenants. But then I'm sure, as a landlord you are perfectly well aware of those laws, hence your determination to remove my uncle from his home.'

Lucy could say nothing. She was too stunned; too appalled. She glanced uncertainly round the table. Verity looked unhappy and upset, and Lucy could see on the faces of the others the interest and speculation Niall Cameron's comments had caused.

It was no secret, of course, that she had inherited the cottage, nor indeed was the state it was in, but, just as she had barely recognised the cottage from Verity's description, so she had hardly been able to recognise herself or her motives in Niall Cameron's denunciation of her.

Eric Barnes...*afraid* of her? She remembered how he had treated her, her eyes blank with disbelief as she turned her head to look at her accuser.

'There seems to have been some misunderstanding,' she told him as calmly as she could. She was not going to argue, to verbally brawl with him here in public, abusing Verity's hospitality, but his accusations could not be allowed to stand.

'I'm glad you understand that,' he told her, deliberately misunderstanding her. 'You might believe that your family's position locally entitles you to behave as you wish, but *I* do not intend to stand by and see my uncle bullied and threatened, just so that you can make a nice fat profit on his home.'

A nice fat profit. Had he *seen* the cottage? Did he have any idea of what it would cost to make it habitable? Did he really expect her or anyone else who knew his uncle to believe the picture he was drawing of Eric Barnes?

She stood up awkwardly, her face white with temper and strain. Turning to Verity, she said fiercely, 'Verity, I am sorry about this. I think I'd better leave.' How *dare* he do this to her? How *dare* he ruin Verity's dinner party like this? How *dare* he try to blacken her reputation? For the first time in her adult life she realised that she was in the grip of an almost uncontrollable surge of temper. Had it been there she could have willingly picked up her soup bowl and tipped the contents over him. She was bitterly, furiously, savagely angry in a way that was totally outside her experience of her own emotions.

And she had to get away now before she gave way to those feelings.

At the other end of the table, Don was trying to speak, saying uncomfortably, 'I think there's been a mistake here, Niall,' but Lucy silenced him, shaking her head.

'No, Don,' she said fiercely. 'Let Mr Cameron say what he thinks. After all, he's obviously extremely well versed in the subject,' she added bitterly.

She refused to allow Verity to persuade her to stay, escaping to her car as quickly as she could. She was, she realised, shaking with temper and lack of self-control.

Oh, God, but she would love to see Niall Cameron's face when he found out the truth about his precious uncle. And about her. He seemed to think she was some kind of wealthy local would-be socialite.

Oh, but the arrogance of the man. And the rudeness! Using Verity's party to attack her. But then honesty made her acknowledge that it *had* been Verity who had first brought up the subject of the cottage and its inhabitant.

She drove home far too fast, too angry to care that she was exceeding the speed limit, finding some small sense of release in driving her car a little too recklessly.

Oh, but she was so angry. She had known from the first moment she had set eyes on him that she wasn't going to like Niall Cameron, but this... She had never, ever imagined anything like this.

She was far, far too wrought up to sleep and impulsively, once she was home, she changed into her jeans, a thick sweater and her trainers. Despite the dark, she was going for a long walk, the only way she knew of ridding herself of the demons of anger and pride that were savaging her.

A tiny corner of her mind told her what she was doing was reckless and dangerous, but she was in no mood to heed them. The whole area was criss-crossed with footpaths, but instinctively her feet chose only one of them.

She knew already where it would take her, and her eyes stung with tears as urgency impelled her, so that she was almost running rather than walking, past the small church where there was a small plaque in memory of her parents, across the small strip of common ground down the lane, and there it was: the house where she had grown up.

An ordinary enough house. Detached, but not particularly large. One of half a dozen down this cul-de-sac, surrounded by fields.

Theirs had been the last house in the row. She stopped outside it, her body trembling with tension, the tears hot and salty in her throat.

How could it have happened? How could anyone have made such vile accusations against her, and in front of her friends, people who knew her, who knew her family? And how many of them would wonder secretly if there weren't some grain of truth in what he was saying? She shivered a little; the tears had stopped now. She could feel the tightness on her face where they had dried.

She felt slightly calmer and dreadfully tired, but coming here had soothed her a little as she had known it would. It was here that she had spent her happy, loved childhood years...here that she had felt safe and protected.

She turned round and began to walk home.

She saw the Discovery the moment she reached home. It was parked beside her own small car. She stopped, tense with fear and sickness as she watched Niall Cameron climbing out of it, but it was too late; he had seen her.

Pride made her walk tensely towards him, her head held high.

He made no comment on her changed appearance but his look registered it, and as he focused on her face she recognised, too late to do anything about it, that he had probably seen the traces of her tears as well.

That knowledge made her glower at him, tilting her chin firmly as she waited for him to speak.

'I've just been speaking with Don,' he told her tersely.

'Oh, yes. Why? Were you demanding that he sacked me?' she asked him acidly.

It gave her a great deal of pleasure to see the angry burn of colour run up under his skin.

'He explained your situation to me,' he continued coldly. 'And it seems that—'

'That what?' Lucy interrupted him sarcastically. 'That I'm not the wealthy money-dominated landlord you described over dinner tonight?'

She made no effort to hide her resentment or her bitterness.

'I have no intention of trying to evict your uncle or to sell the cottage,' she told him fiercely. 'Even if it were in a fit state to be sold, which it most certainly is not.'

'I agree,' he told her tightly. 'In fact—'

'In fact what? In fact, that's why you're here now...to demand your pound of flesh, or rather your saintly, timid uncle's pound of flesh.'

Lucy was well into her stride now, half of her marvelling, half of her appalled by where her temper was taking her. Never had she felt like this or behaved like this before.

'I'm surprised I didn't guess the relationship between you,' she told him acidly. 'I ought to have recognised the resemblance immediately. You're obviously two of a kind.'

She heard his indrawn breath and knew that she had pushed him too far, but she didn't care. How dared he have said the things he had said to her?

Inwardly she wept with pain and shame over them. Inwardly she was bitterly, deeply hurt, but she would never, ever allow him to see that.

'Now just a minute,' he began. He was coming towards her and immediately Lucy panicked, stepping back from him, tensing as she saw the anger darkening his eyes. He reached for her, grabbing hold of her, while she tried to pull away, demanding to be let go.

No man had ever touched her in anger...no man had ever taken hold of her against her will. No man had ever imposed himself on her senses as this man was doing, and she fought frantically against him, driven by fear and panic.

'For God's sake, you little fool. *Will* you keep still?' she heard him saying, and then he was dragging her against him and she could smell the hot male scent of him, feel the anger and power in his body.

She reacted instinctively to it, lifting her hand, hitting him as hard as she could, feeling the stinging sensation in her palm as it connected with his face.

The sound of the blow shocked her into sharp awareness. A feeling of sick dismay drowned out her fear and anger. How could she have behaved in such an uncontrolled way, even with such provocation?

She was aware that he was still holding her, but

it no longer seemed to matter. She made tiredly to pull herself free. She would have to apologise, she acknowledged miserably, and then she realised that he wasn't going to let her go, and as she looked uncertainly up at him she saw that, unlike hers, his anger still burned furiously.

'My God, I'm not going to let you get away with that,' he told her thickly, and then before she could stop him he twisted both her hands behind her back, holding her imprisoned frighteningly easily with one hand, while he used the other to hold the back of her neck.

And even then she had no realisation, no warning of what he intended to do. She was too taken off guard by his physical imprisonment of her to realise what was going to happen.

All she did know was that she had to apologise to him now before the whole thing got completely out of control. She looked up at him and her heart suddenly missed a couple of beats, shock arcing through her as she finally recognised his intention.

She tried to stop him, but her denial, her husky, 'No, please don't...' was stifled in her throat by the savagery of his kiss.

No one had ever kissed her in anger before. The shock of it, the shame of it, made her tremble with violent rejection. She knew exactly what the kiss was, recognised immediately its punishment and contempt. There was no passion in it, no desire. She could feel his anger stifling her, possessing her, destroying her. She felt sick and giddy, almost close to fainting, and, as though he recognised it, he suddenly let her go.

She was trembling visibly, too shocked to even attempt to conceal from him how she felt. In an automatic, almost childlike gesture, she touched her mouth with her fingers, tears burning like acid in her throat.

He had released her completely, and she started to step back from him, too terrified to take her eyes off him in case...

She heard him curse, and her whole body flinched. She stopped moving, tensing like a terrified animal, cringing when she felt his hands reaching out for her a second time.

This time she couldn't even plead with him not to touch her. She was too terrified, frozen with shock and disbelief.

Her eyes wide open, she saw him lower his head, sickness eddying in her stomach as she waited for the cold anger of his kiss, but instead his mouth felt shockingly warm, its touch light, delicate, somehow almost comforting.

Comforting! She trembled violently, dizzy and confused. He was still kissing her, his mouth moving gently on hers. Her thoughts had slowed to a nervous crawl; she seemed incapable of moving…it crossed her mind that she should pull away, that he was only holding her very lightly, but she was afraid that if she did that punishing, savage kiss would begin again. It was much better to stay where she was, to remain quiescent and still. But she had to breathe, and somehow she couldn't do so without opening her mouth, and when she did she shuddered in disbelief. It must be because her mouth was sore that it felt so sensitive, so…sensitised by the gentle pressure of his. Yes, that must be why her lips were clinging to his, why she was trembling so violently, why she suddenly wanted to close her eyes, to move closer to him, to…

Fiercely she pulled herself out of his arms, and this time he let her go. She couldn't believe it… couldn't believe she had actually wanted… invited… She took a deep gulping breath of air. She must be going crazy, losing her mind; there couldn't be any other explanation.

She heard him saying something to her, but she couldn't bear to listen. Before he could stop her she turned on her heel, almost running towards the building.

CHAPTER THREE

EVEN now Lucy couldn't believe what had happened, couldn't accept what she had actually felt. She *must* have imagined it. But how was it possible to *imagine* that kind of reaction, that kind of awareness, that kind of arousal? And she *had* been aroused, no matter how much she hated to admit it.

She shuddered, wrapping her arms tightly round her body as though she could somehow squeeze out and destroy the sensations she had felt. They were gone now, thank goodness, and if she closed her eyes and tried to remember...to imagine...but no, she wasn't going to be foolish enough to do that. Better by far to cling instead to the memory of that first angry, punishing kiss than to allow herself to dwell on how it had felt to have Niall Cameron's mouth moving slowly and gently against hers, to feel her body slowly coming to life, to feel a sweet, heady need to move closer to him.

And she *had* felt those things, she acknowledged shudderingly; she had felt them.

In the distance she could hear the telephone start

to ring, but she could not summon the strength of will to move in order to answer it.

She let it ring, the strength of the effect Niall Cameron had had on her senses still so powerful that it dulled her awareness of everything else.

The phone had stopping ringing. She stared vacantly into the darkness of her now silent flat. *How* had it happened? How *could* it have happened that she had experienced such sensations? Was it something that had been unleashed by the intensity of her anger, some odd by-product of that emotion?

She felt seared, degraded almost by her own reaction to him, and *he* had felt it too. She had seen it in his eyes, that brief dark flash of comprehension, registering what was happening to her, while her own heart seemed to turn over with shock and disbelief.

It was a long time before she felt able to get up and prepare for bed. Her brain teemed with thoughts, with fears, while her heart hammered anxiously within her chest.

He was not her type. She didn't even like him. She *disliked* him, in fact. And, if it weren't enough that he was Eric Barnes's nephew, he was also emotionally and morally committed to someone else.

But he had still kissed her.

In *anger*, she reminded herself fiercely. He had kissed her in *anger*. She wasn't going to let herself remember that second kiss; she dared not. It must be forgotten, pushed out of her consciousness as though it had never happened.

By morning she had managed, just, to convince herself that it had been a mixture of anger and intensity which was responsible for her foolish and mistaken belief that she had actually experienced physical desire for Niall Cameron. The price of that conviction had been a virtually sleepless night, but it was worth it, she told herself as she used the discipline she had taught herself to force her tired body out of bed and into its normal Sunday-morning routine.

She could have had her Sunday papers delivered like the other residents of the building, but instead she preferred to exercise her body by either walking or running the two miles into the town to collect them herself.

This morning, despite her tiredness, she decided she would run, and as she stood under the cool shower, which she hoped would help her to wake up, she refused to admit that she was perhaps trying to punish her body for last night's treachery.

They were having a pleasantly mild spring, and so she dressed comfortably for her run, pulling a thin cotton T-shirt and a pair of cotton shorts over her underwear.

Her skin was too pale to tan well, but it had the

peachy warm glow of healthy, well-toned flesh, and, even if Lucy herself was unaware of her body's feminine sensuality, others were not, several male drivers automatically slowing down just a fraction as they saw her.

Lucy never normally paid much attention to the traffic, but she was instantly aware of the two-toned Discovery coming down the road towards her. Her body tensed, tiny, fizzing, dizzying impulses shooting from her nerve-endings. Her body trembled, her smooth pace losing its rhythm, her chest so tight that she could hardly breathe. She could see the driver of the Discovery now, and it wasn't Niall Cameron. It wasn't even his vehicle, she recognised, but it was too late, the damage was done. Her concentration had gone; her body was trembling as though she had run ten miles and not barely one. That hot, frantic surge of adrenalin-based panic had gone, leaving her drained of energy and willpower.

She walked the rest of the way into town, trying to run only once, but the instant she did so she trembled so much that she had to stop.

She bought her papers and then walked home with them. Sunday morning with her papers, eating her breakfast outside on her small private patio if it was warm enough, was one of her special private pleasures, but this morning, despite the sunshine, despite the fresh green smell of growing things, it was impossible for her to experience the enjoyment these simple pleasures normally brought her.

She tasted the orange juice she had just squeezed and almost dropped the glass as the acid liquid stung her mouth, finding a tiny little cut she herself had not even known was there. Now, as she touched it with her tongue-tip, she was sharply conscious of how it had been caused. Her heart started hammering against her ribs, and totally against her will she was suddenly reliving the whole thing; the anger of Niall Cameron's punishing kiss…the way he had held her and looked at her, the way he had kissed her that second time, his mouth suddenly so warm and tender that…

She reached angrily for her coffee-cup, but her hand was shaking so much that she had to put it down again, her coffee untouched. She was going completely crazy, she told herself despairingly. She *must* stop thinking about it…about *him*…

The phone rang and she stared at it, her body tensing, her eyes huge with dread. It couldn't be Niall Cameron. He had no reason to ring her… None at all, she told herself sharply.

Even so, it was several seconds before she managed to cross the room and pick up the receiver.

'Oh, there you are!' she heard Verity exclaiming. 'I was just about to hang up.'

'Verity.'

Did her voice sound as high and strained to Verity as it did to her?

'I'm sorry, I should have rung you to thank you for last night.'

'I tried to ring you last night,' Verity told her. 'Lucy, I promise you I had no idea that Niall was related to Eric Barnes. Don told me I must ring and apologise to you. I can't *think* where Niall got the idea from that you're persecuting his uncle. Don spoke to him about it after you'd gone and tried to explain how difficult Eric is being. Of course, we all know that none of it is your fault, and Don told Niall as much.'

Lucy let Verity run on, outwardly silent but inwardly cringing with misery and distaste. The last thing she wanted was for anyone to plead with Niall Cameron on her behalf. She was perfectly capable of defending her own actions did she feel they needed defending, and she could all too easily imagine the sort of things Don would have said to him.

'Of course, once Niall realised the truth he said immediately that he would apologise to you,' Verity was saying. 'Which is just as well, because it would have been dreadfully difficult for Don if some kind of feud had developed between the two of you, what with him being one of Don's clients and you working for Don.'

What was Verity trying to tell her? Lucy wondered bleakly. That for Don's sake she must accept
not only Niall Cameron's apology, but also, pub-
licly at least, be seen to accept the man himself?
Did her feelings not matter at all? she wondered
bitterly. Was she supposed to simply smile and pretend that she didn't care about the way she had been
insulted?

'Of course, as Don said to Niall, he accepts that
the cottage badly needs repairing. He told Niall that
you yourself had admitted as much.'

Lucy could feel her muscles tensing as anger
took over from pain.

Was she merely imagining it, or was Verity now
actually implying that somehow *she* was at fault in
not doing anything about the state of the cottage?
Verity knew as well as she did exactly what the
situation was; that it wasn't from any lack of awareness of her obligations that nothing had been done,
but simply because she did not have the money.

Had Don told Niall Cameron that as well? Had
he told him that, far from being the pampered,
wealthy woman he seemed to think her, she was in
fact wholly dependent on her salary for income?

She had seen last night at dinner that Niall
Cameron seemed to think that they were still living
in the era when her family had been extensive local

landowners. No doubt Don had put him right about that as well.

'Of course, Niall fully accepts now that you never had any intention of trying to sell the cottage, but I had to admit I can understand how distressing it must have been for him to discover that his uncle was living in such dreadful conditions.'

Lucy digested this comment in silence, but inwardly she wondered acidly why, if Niall Cameron had found it so distressing, he had not done something to help his uncle. After all, he had the money.

'I suppose, with Niall's side of the family having lost all contact with Eric, and Niall only just having in fact discovered Eric's existence, it must have come as quite a shock to find him living in that kind of squalor. It seems that Eric quarrelled with his family as a young man and that it was only recently, following his own father's death, that Niall learned of his existence.'

After their conversation had ended Lucy put down the receiver and glared angrily at her now unwanted breakfast. Her stomach was churning far too much for her to be able to eat. Everything Verity had said to her had underlined the subtle changes that had taken place in her friend's attitude towards the problem of the cottage.

From supporting Lucy completely, Verity now seemed to be implying that she, Lucy, was somehow guilty of turning her back on her moral responsibilities.

Not that Verity had said so outright. Outwardly she had still continued to support Lucy's position, but sensitively Lucy had caught the undertow of doubt in Verity's words, and she knew quite well who had put that doubt into her friend's mind.

Did Niall Cameron think she *wanted* to be in this position? she wondered bitterly. Did he really believe for one moment that if she *had* had the money to effect the repairs she would not do so immediately?

First thing tomorrow morning she would approach the bank again and ask them if they could rethink their decision not to lend her the money for the repairs, she decided tensely.

Although the large grounds surrounding the house were maintained by contractors, the ground-floor patios were the responsibility of the individual tenants. Lucy's was her own design, and comprised of old bricks set in a herringbone pattern. It was surrounded by a low wall with steps set in it. Every corner overflowed with terra-cotta pots, brimful of plants. More pots decorated the steps; these still held her previous autumn's planting of dwarf bulbs and ivies. The bulb's flowering season was almost over, and it was time to replant them.

Ordinarily the sight of them would have motivated her to make a trip to one of the local garden centres, where she could browse and daydream at will, planning her new season's colour scheme, but today she was too tense and angry. It was impossible for her to think of anything other than the cottage and the problems it was causing her.

Because Niall Cameron was a part of that problem it was perhaps only natural that she should think of him as well. And that was the only reason she *was* thinking of him, Lucy assured herself as she cleared away her untouched breakfast.

Halfway through the morning Tom rang her to say that he had got the children and asking her if she would like to accompany them on a visit to Chester Zoo and a trip on the river afterwards.

Firmly Lucy declined. They were Tom's children and it was only right that when they were with him they should have his undivided attention, especially since they were so young.

In the afternoon, even though she already knew the answer, she sat down with her bank statements, her few share certificates, her insurance policy and anything else that might be worth a few pounds, and tried for the umpteenth time to discover some way in which she could raise the money for the repairs to the cottage.

It was no use. There was only one real way. To sell her home. Even in this present depressed market, it would probably sell. The development was a one-off; the builder had originally planned to build separate blocks of flats on the same piece of land, but planning permission had been withheld, with the result that the apartments were set in what was almost a mini-parkland. No, she would have no trouble selling, but once she had sold, once she had used her capital to repair the cottage, she would not be able to buy herself another home. Her salary, while quite good, would never cover the interest payments she would be required to make, even if she could find a bank or building society to lend the money to her.

She would own the cottage, of course, but she could hardly live there…not while it was tenanted, which meant that she would have to find rented accommodation herself…or, rather, she would have to find someone willing to let a room to her, because that was as much as she would be able to afford.

Stoically she stared out of the window. There was no point in feeling sorry for herself. Facts were facts. Neither was there any point in wishing that Emily had had the forethought to will her property to someone else, preferably Eric Barnes himself, she reflected acidly.

First thing in the morning she would ring the bank. Her heart sank as she tidied the papers on her desk. She suspected that she already knew what their response was going to be, but she had to try.

'*YOU* must have arrived early.'

Lucy tried to smile as Don walked into her office. It was just gone nine, and she had been here since eight.

'You're not still worrying about the cottage, are you?' Don asked her as she handed him the post. 'I've had a word with Niall Cameron and explained the position to him. Did Verity—?'

'She rang me yesterday,' Lucy interrupted him. 'Niall Cameron did call round on Saturday after the party.'

'Yes, he said he intended to apologise to you,' Don told her. 'It was obvious from his comments that there had been some kind of misunderstanding. Of course, I can accept that it must have come as a shock to him, discovering the way his uncle was living, but, as I explained to him, that wasn't *your* fault...your cousin—'

'That doesn't alter the fact that the state of the cottage is now my responsibility, though, does it?' Lucy challenged him quietly.

Don was a kind man, and it hurt her to see the way he avoided looking directly at her. He fidgeted with the post for a few seconds and said uncomfortably, 'It's a very unfortunate situation all round,

Lucy. We all know that you simply don't have that kind of money. Eric Barnes is somewhat eccentric. He seems to have this bee in his bonnet about your family and what he imagines is the wealth you've inherited from them. Privately I think he's been living on his own for too long. Like a lot of old people, he's developed some very fixed ideas he won't relinquish.

'As a matter of fact, I'm seeing Niall this morning. He wants to discuss some alterations to his company's financial structure.'

And to further poison Don's mind against *her*? Lucy wondered bitterly, but she didn't say anything. Her pride would not let her.

She rang the bank while Don was looking at the post, and managed to make an appointment for her lunch-hour.

By the time she got there she felt almost sick with nerves. The manager was new to the area, a woman in her early forties, whom Lucy already knew was extremely professional in her attitude towards her work.

She welcomed Lucy with a smile and invited her to sit down.

Since she already knew the situation with the cottage, Lucy only needed to recap briefly before asking if there was any way at all in which the bank could assist her.

Daphne Irving listened gravely.

'In ordinary circumstances, if the cottage were—
shall we say?—a little more structurally sound, and
if it did not have a sitting tenant, we could probably
advance the money against a charge over it, but
these are very difficult times in the property market
and, given the fact that the property is tenanted and
that there is no way it could be sold after renovation
to repay the loan, I'm afraid—'

'But what about my apartment?' Lucy interrupted her quickly. 'I don't have a mortgage on
that.'

Daphne Irving sighed.

'Lucy, I'd like to be able to help, but the bank
sets certain rules. The interest rate on the kind of
money you need would make the repayments far
too large for you to finance from your salary. My
dear, you couldn't even cover the interest, never
mind make any capital repayments.'

It was only what Lucy had expected to hear, what
she had known in her heart to be the truth, but she
had still not been able to stop herself from hoping.
Like a child wishing for the impossible to happen,
she told herself bitterly as she walked back to the
office.

On the way she passed an estate agent's office
and hastily averted her gaze. How *could* she part
with her apartment? It was her home, her security...

She could feel the panic filling her at the very thought; the fear that was part of her legacy from her parents' death.

For the next two days Lucy worried the problem over and over in her mind, looking for a solution she knew she would not find. There was only one thing she could do, only one way she could raise the money to effect the repairs, repairs which her pride was now insisting had to be made.

She was going to have to sell the flat.

She didn't tell anyone about her decision. After all, why should she? In her heart of hearts she knew she hadn't done so because she dreaded facing their pity. People like Don and Verity, kind as they were, had no real conception of what it was like to be in her position.

And neither did the Niall Camerons of this world. Well, he would be pleased. He would be getting his pound of flesh, or, rather, his uncle would, and she would die sooner than allow either of them to know what it was costing her.

She was only thankful that Niall Cameron hadn't made any further attempt to get in touch with her. But then why *should* he? No doubt he thought he had made adequate reparation for his unwarranted attack on her. And, of course, he had the added satisfaction of taking away with him the knowledge that she... No...no, she wasn't going to think about

that, she told herself sickly. It was better to pretend
that it had simply never happened…that she had
imagined the whole thing. It was better…safer, in
fact, to tell herself that there had never been any
second kiss, and to hold fast instead to that first
one.

Yes, she was thankful that she had not seen him
again. Not that she was afraid of him in any
way…or, indeed, afraid of herself. What had happened, that shocking *frisson* of sensation, of need,
had quite obviously been a total aberration, something which could never happen again, and of
course she had no fear of its ever doing so. Why
should she, when she had far more important things
to occupy her mind…things like losing her home?

She had made up her mind. There was no going
back now, and, just to prove it, this weekend she
would visit Eric Barnes herself and tell him that the
repairs were soon going to be put in hand.

It would be a long process, of course; there
would be estimates to get, and before any work
could be done her flat would have to be sold.

She was, she acknowledged, going to have a very
busy summer.

And a very unhappy one, a small inner voice
added, but she silenced it, knowing that she could
not afford to listen to it.

CHAPTER FOUR

'Go away. I don't want to see you.'

Lucy grimaced, clenching her teeth, trying to hold on to her temper.

She had arrived at the cottage five minutes ago, and so far Eric Barnes was refusing to let her in.

'Mr Barnes, it's Lucy Howard,' she tried again. 'I need to talk with you about the cottage. About the repairs.'

Silence.

Lucy waited tensely.

The door opened a couple of inches and Eric Barnes peered out at her.

'Mr Barnes, I need to speak to you about the repairs,' she said firmly, and walked towards the door.

To her relief, he stood back and allowed her into the house. As she had been on her first visit, she was immediately aware of the stale, unpleasant smell of the air inside the cottage. Despite the sunshine outside, it felt cold, and she knew she could smell damp.

As Eric Barnes turned away from her to walk down the narrow hall she could see the patches of damp staining the walls. The cottage really wasn't fit for anyone to live in, she acknowledged, but she knew that the local authority had offered to rehouse the old man and that he had refused.

'Seeing sense now, are you?' he pronounced triumphantly as he opened the door into the kitchen. 'Now that that nephew of mine's told you a thing or two.'

Lucy gritted her teeth. She must not allow him to upset or hurt her.

'You're all the same, your kind,' he told her nastily. 'Think you can treat people how you like. There are laws now to protect old folks like me. I dare say I could even claim compensation from you.' He coughed theatrically. 'It's damaged my chest, you know, having to live in this place.'

Lucy fought to subdue the panic rising inside her. *Could* he claim compensation? She really had no idea, but she suspected she knew who was responsible for making him think so.

She tried as calmly as she could to explain to him that she would need to obtain estimates for the work that needed to be done, and that it might be some months before the repairs could actually start.

'And what's to become of me once this place is full of workmen? Have you thought of that?' he demanded. 'Like as not, they'll have to take the roof off, and then there's the drains... Needs new ones, it does.'

He was right, Lucy realised weakly. He could not possibly continue to live here once the work started.

'Don't think I don't know what you're up to,' he accused her. 'You just want me out of here so that you can sell the place over my head. Well, I'm not going.'

Indignantly Lucy told him that he was wrong; that she simply wanted to have the cottage made properly habitable.

'You think because I'm old that I'm stupid,' he challenged her. His voice had suddenly risen, and developed a high, almost frightened note to it, so at odds to his previously fiercely aggressive tone that Lucy was too taken aback to make any response.

'You just want me out of here, don't you?' he continued in the same tremulous voice. 'Well, I'm not afraid of you, so don't you go thinking I am. I might be an old man, but I'm not alone...not any more.'

'What are *you* doing here?'

Lucy whirled round, her face ashen as she saw Niall Cameron standing in the open doorway.

When had *he* arrived, and why hadn't she heard him? He was dressed in jeans and a faded rugby shirt which looked uncomfortably as though he might actually at one time have played in it.

As he walked to stand with his uncle Lucy saw that he was wearing trainers, which explained why she had not heard him, but, unlike her, Eric Barnes had not been standing with his back to the open door, which probably explained the sudden abrupt change in his voice and his manner, Lucy recognised bitterly.

Now, with both of them standing opposite her, she refused to allow herself to be intimidated.

'I came to see Mr Barnes, as I have a perfect right to do. After all, this *is* my property.'

She flushed as she saw the contempt in Niall Cameron's eyes.

'In your shoes, that would be an admission I'd prefer not to make,' he told her, giving a comprehensive look at the kitchen.

Lucy flinched as she read the expression on his face. The kitchen was an appalling sight.

There were no kitchen units to speak of, just a chipped stone sink and a metal cupboard standing against one wall. There was an old Formica-covered table in the middle of the floor; the three chairs with it had torn vinyl seats. The linoleum on the floor was filthy and ripped in places. There was a huge patch of black fungus-covered damp on one wall, and Lucy knew that the thought of eating or drinking anything prepared in this kitchen would make her physically ill.

She had no idea how Eric Barnes had managed to survive here for so long, but she suspected that his stubborn contrariness must have had something to do with it.

'I have only owned the cottage for the last four months,' she told him, trying to defend herself, determined not to let him browbeat her. 'And, as far as I know, it is *not* a landlord's duty to provide a cleaning service.'

It was an unkind remark and one she would never normally have made. She could see quite clearly from the angry colour that burned along Niall's face what he thought of it.

'My uncle is virtually eighty years old,' he told her quietly, so quietly that his restraint made her flush with guilt and shame. 'And this is hardly the easiest of places to keep clean, given its primitive facilities.'

Lucy longed to retort that had his uncle had any sense he could have been comfortably rehoused in an easy-to-run bungalow in the council's complex, but she bit on her tongue, telling herself that she was not going to be pressured into behaving vindictively.

'And, as for the fact that you have only owned the property for four months, you surely knew it existed. Your cousin, I understand, spent the last fifteen years of her life in a private home. Surely you could have made some attempt to check that the property was habitable?'

'Fifteen years ago I was eleven years old,' Lucy told him, her determination to remain restrained vanishing.

She wasn't going to explain to him that Emily's senility had been such that, coupled with her parents' death, she had not even realised that Emily still owned the cottage until her cousin had died.

No doubt, in the normal course of events, her father would have obtained a power of attorney and dealt with the problem, but at seventeen, newly orphaned, the last thing that had occurred to her had been to check to see if a distant cousin, to whom she had only paid the occasional duty visit with her parents, still owned a cottage Lucy was only vaguely aware existed.

'And I repeat my original question. What are you doing here?'

Lucy opened her mouth to tell him, but Eric Barnes forestalled her, using the quavery, hesitant voice Lucy was sure he adopted specially for his nephew's benefit, and he said quickly, 'She wants to get me out of here, Niall. She came here, spinning some story of getting the repairs done, and then she told me that I'll have to move out. I know what she's up to. She wants to get rid of me...to sell this place.'

He was becoming so agitated that even Lucy was almost convinced that his apprehension was genuine, and she could see all too plainly that Niall was completely convinced.

He placed a reassuring hand on his uncle's shoulder, and gave him a gentle smile. Seeing it, Lucy swallowed hard. Her throat was suddenly constricted and her eyes stung. What on earth was the matter with her?

Gentleness or indeed anything else from this man was the last thing she wanted.

He turned to her, the gentleness gone, a hard contempt taking its place.

'Don assured me that you had no intention of selling,' he told her curtly.

'I don't,' Lucy confirmed. 'As I was trying to explain to your uncle, I came here simply to tell him that I intended to have the repairs done, but that I would need to get estimates, and that it would be some time—'

'A change of heart, isn't it?' Niall interrupted her flatly, his eyes hard and watchful. 'A week ago you were claiming that you couldn't afford to have the repairs done.'

Lucy pressed her lips firmly together. She owed

him no explanation of what she was doing, and she certainly wasn't going to give him one.

'I don't suppose my reminder that there are legal remedies open to my uncle as a tenant of this property has any bearing on your change of mind, has it?'

Insufferable…hateful…loathsome man, Lucy fumed, but she kept her thoughts and her anger to herself.

'No, as a matter of fact, it doesn't,' she told him coldly, and then, tilting her chin, she added, 'I don't respond to bullying or aggression of any kind, Mr Cameron,' and as she forced herself to look at him she realised too late that he might think she was not just referring to the verbal threats he had made at the dinner party, but to the physical way he had threatened her later.

Her whole body burned with heat and misery. *Was* he thinking, gloating, that, while she might not have responded to his physical aggression, she had certainly and unmistakably responded to the kiss that had followed?

The humiliation of that knowledge would never leave her…never.

It ought to be *him* she felt contempt for and not herself, she told herself wildly. After all, *he* was committed to another woman. He had no right…no right at all to have kissed her the way he had.

'She just wants to get me out of here...that's what she's really after.' Eric Barnes's thin whine drew Niall's attention back to the old man.

'Is this true?' he demanded fiercely.

Tiredly Lucy shook her head.

'No. In fact, it was your uncle who brought up the fact that he couldn't stay here while the repairs were taking place.'

She didn't want to say that, until he had, she had not really thought beyond her misery at having to sell her flat to finance the work, and that the last thing on her mind had been what would happen to her tenant while they were being done.

'She wants to get me out of here and into some old folks' home,' Eric Barnes continued. 'I know what she's up to. A good hotel, that's where I should go. Somewhere where an old man can be properly looked after, not half bullied to death. I know what happens in these places. Plenty folk go into them, but there's only one way they come out.'

Lucy couldn't conceal her alarm. She felt sick with the shock of it... A hotel...and she could tell that Eric Barnes would expect her to pay for it. Was she legally liable to do so? she wondered frantically. How *could* she afford that kind of additional expense?

'Nothing like that will be necessary,' she heard Niall Cameron saying calmly.

She waited for the blow to fall, for him to tell her, and to enjoy telling her, that she would be legally liable for his uncle's hotel bills while the repairs were being done, and then to her astonishment she heard him saying instead, 'There's no need for you to worry about that, Uncle Eric. You can stay with me.'

Lucy almost felt as though she could be sick with relief, but when she looked at Eric Barnes she could see that he was far from pleased by Niall's suggestion.

Niall was obviously aware of it as well, because he was frowning slightly.

'Don't you like the idea?' he asked.

'It isn't that,' Eric assured him, adopting the quavery voice which had disappeared while he had been announcing that he was not going to be forced into any 'home'. 'I just don't want to be a trouble to you, that's all.'

'You won't be,' Niall assured him positively, and then he turned to Lucy and asked her coolly, 'When do you expect the men to actually start work?'

'I'm not sure yet,' Lucy hedged. She had no intention of telling him that nothing could be done until she had sold her flat.

She saw from his face that he suspected that she had no intention of having the work done at all, and told him quickly, 'There will be estimates to get first, and a lot will depend on when the contractors can actually do the work.'

'So it could be several months, then?' he asked, and she nodded. 'Well, once you *do* have some firm dates, perhaps you would let me know.'

Was he warning her that he intended to make sure she followed through with her promise to have the work done? Well, he had no need, she reflected bitterly as she drove away from the cottage ten minutes later.

As she headed for home she wondered a little unkindly how his girlfriend would react to having Eric Barnes living with them. She also wondered with equally grim satisfaction how long Eric would manage to keep up the façade of fragility and weakness he had portrayed so successfully this afternoon once he was actually living with Niall.

Of the two of them, she wasn't quite sure which one she liked the less, but on balance she decided it must be Niall. So why, then, later on in the evening, did she have an odd, unguarded memory of the gentleness in Niall's face as he had reassured his uncle, and why did the knowledge of that gentleness clog her throat with tears and make her heart ache with a pain she didn't want to recognise?

LUCY LOOKED unhappily around her small sitting-room; most of her furniture had come from her parents' home and, though she had not been able to keep everything—the flat was too small for that—the things she had kept all had special memories attached to them. There was the pretty Edwardian nest of tables her mother had told her had originally been a wedding present to Lucy's great-grandmother; there was the early-Victorian dining table and its matching chairs, the table so large that, even with its extra leaves removed, it occupied most of the space in her small dining-room; the heavy Knole sofa which she had had re-covered in a pretty lemon damask fabric; the chair which had always been her father's favourite; the glass-fronted bureau cum bookcase which she had been told was an extremely valuable piece of late Regency furniture but which she knew she could never part with because it held so many precious memories.

She remembered her mother opening the glass doors and showing her the small delicate china coffee-cup with its matching saucer, a christening present to Lucy from a great-aunt. The cup and saucer were still there, along with the other pieces of china her mother had collected.

Lucy suspected that, put together, the contents of her flat would probably be worth as much as the flat itself, but there was no way she could ever sell them. They were her last link with her parents...with her childhood.

Once her flat was sold they would have to go into storage. She opened the glass doors to the bookcase and gently removed her christening cup and saucer, touching its surface with her fingertips and closing her eyes, willing herself to mentally conjure up the memory of her mother, the sound of her voice, the perfume she had always worn, but instead the image dominating her senses was that of Niall Cameron.

Her eyes snapped open, her mouth trembling a little. Niall Cameron was the last person she wanted to think about. It frightened her that he had managed somehow to infiltrate her thoughts so much that he had actually penetrated here, the place that held her most precious memories and where she always instinctively sought the solace of their comfort.

Now it seemed that even that comfort was to be denied to her.

She shivered, tears burning her eyes, the fragile cup rattling dangerously on its saucer. She turned back to the cabinet, opening it, her hands shaking as she restored the cup and saucer to their place.

It was too late for second thoughts now. She had already seen the estate agent and the flat would soon be officially up for sale.

She wasn't going to cry, she told herself fiercely. What possible good would it do? She must hold on instead to the shame and the anger she had felt when Niall Cameron had virtually accused her of trying to evade her responsibilities towards his uncle.

It should not, after all, be hard. In fact, it should have been very easy, but unnervingly when she *did* conjure up a mental image of him it was not the Niall Cameron who had denounced her with such contempt and anger who filled her thoughts, but the Niall who had stood so caringly, so protectively next to his uncle, the Niall Cameron who had looked at her in the darkness of the car park, who had touched her face with gentle fingertips and her mouth with tender lips, who had kissed her, however briefly, as though he regretted his earlier unkindness, as though he wished to comfort and cherish her, as though he knew how cruelly his earlier coldness had struck at the most vulnerable female core of her and had wanted to make amends for it.

No. No.

The denial screamed through her mind as she pressed her fist to her mouth to silence the actual words.

That kiss hadn't happened, could not have happened. He was a man she didn't even like, could not possibly like, even if he had not been committed to someone else. Why was she wasting time even thinking about him when she had so much else to do?

Now that the flat was officially in the hands of the estate agent, she must start contacting builders. That, of course, would mean having to contact Eric Barnes again, something she would just have to steel herself to do, she told herself firmly.

'LUCY, are you OK?'

Lucy forced herself to smile as she fibbed quickly, 'Yes, I'm fine, Don.'

'Well, you don't look it,' her boss told her with candour. 'You're losing weight, and you look as though you aren't sleeping properly. Not working you too hard, am I?'

She smiled properly then. Don was a considerate employer, and, although there were times when because they were busy she did have to work extra hours, she enjoyed her job so much that it never seemed onerous.

'No, of course you're not,' she assured him.

She turned back to her desk, assuming that the conversation was over, but to her disquiet Don continued quietly, 'You aren't still worrying about this business of the cottage, are you?'

'I'm concerned about it, naturally,' Lucy told him, pausing and then choosing her words carefully. She had decided not to tell her friends of her decision to sell her flat. Ultimately they would have to know, of course, but she had no wish for anyone to accuse her of trying to attract people's sympathy. Time enough for others to know once the flat was actually sold.

'It *has* been on my mind,' she admitted cautiously, knowing that Don would not believe her if she denied any concern.

'The best thing all round would be for Eric Barnes to move in with Niall,' Don commented. 'That way you'd be free of any obligation to do anything about the cottage.'

Lucy gave him a tight smile. Judging from Eric Barnes's reaction when Niall had suggested he stay with him while the repairs were being done, Lucy did not think the old man would react well to any suggestion that he lived permanently with his nephew, and she certainly did not think that Niall Cameron would want to do anything to help her— far from it.

'Perhaps Mr Cameron and his…his partner prefer not to share their home with a third party,' Lucy commented quietly.

Don's eyebrows lifted.

'Mr Cameron… That's a bit formal, isn't it?' Without waiting for any response, he added, 'It might be worthwhile someone having a word with him, you know, suggesting that he could—'

'No.'

Lucy's response was immediate and sharp. She saw the surprise in Don's eyes and the thoughtful frown creasing his forehead as he looked at her.

'I...I don't think that would be a good idea, Don,' she amended less fiercely. 'I suspect that Eric Barnes prefers living on his own, and...and, to be honest with you...I'd prefer not to involve anyone else in what, after all, is my responsibility.'

She held her breath, praying that Don would accept her statement and not press her any further. She knew he meant well, but the last thing she wanted was for anyone to start suing Niall Cameron for charity on her behalf. The very last thing. She felt sick with anger and pride at the very thought.

'Well, it was only an idea,' Don told her calmly. He had started to read the post, and lifted his head from one of the letters to smile humorously at her.

'It seems you made quite an impression on Monsieur Jacques Fèvre,' he told her. 'He's written to me, in English, telling me how impressed he was with your professionalism, and that he hopes to meet you again the next time I have business in France.'

This was much more comfortable ground for her, and Lucy grinned back at him.

'I know what's going through your mind,' she said, laughing at him, 'but you're wrong. Monsieur

Fèvre is at least sixty years old, plump and bald, and possessed of an extremely French wife and at least a dozen grandchildren.'

In fact, she had enjoyed meeting the Fèvre family, who had welcomed her warmly into their home, pressing her to return to visit them, not on business but as their guest.

She might actually have contemplated doing so, but holidays were something that were going to be out for her in the foreseeable future.

They had an extremely busy day, and Lucy was still hard at work when Don announced that he had to leave early.

'Verity and I are having dinner with Niall tonight at the farm, and Verity's warned me not to be late. Why don't you have an early night as well? You look tired.'

Lucy shook her head.

'I want to finish these projections for the Simmons account. Paul Simmons was on the phone this morning. The bank have been pressing him for them, and I promised I'd have them ready for him to collect in the morning.'

So Niall had invited Don and Verity to the farm. There was no reason why that should suddenly underline and heighten her own solitude, no reason at all. She was single because she chose to be, and, as far as she was concerned, it was far better to be

alone than to be involved with a man like Niall
Cameron who might be kissing someone else the
moment she was not there to be with him.

She worked until almost eight, and it was only
when she finally locked the office door behind her
that she acknowledged that she could have left earlier, that she had deliberately dragged out her work
a little because she was reluctant to go home.

But why should she be? Her home was her haven; she had never experienced this reluctance to
return to it before. Why should she do so now?
After all, it was not as though she was not used to
her solitude, to going home, knowing there would
not be anyone there waiting for her.

Perhaps she ought to get herself a cat, she decided wryly, and then abruptly remembered that she
couldn't...that not even that small choice was hers
to make because all too soon she would not have a
home to share with any kind of pet. Landladies
were notorious for not welcoming people with an-
imals, weren't they?

Stop it, she told herself fiercely; stop feeling
sorry for yourself. It won't do any good.

'VERITY.'

Lucy tried to smile as she answered the phone.
The estate agent had just left. He had been round
to measure up the flat, and he had told her quite

frankly that, while it was excellently maintained and decorated, in the present financial climate she might have to accept a sum lower than it was actually worth to achieve a quick sale.

'I wondered if you fancied coming shopping with me this afternoon,' Verity asked her. 'There's this wonderful shop in Knutsford, and I desperately need a new dress.'

New clothes were the last thing Lucy could afford, but an afternoon spent with Verity might help to keep her mind off her problems.

Unfortunately when Verity picked her up an hour later the first person she mentioned was Niall Cameron.

'You know, we had dinner with him the other night,' she chattered as she drove toward Knutsford.

Lucy nodded.

'Well, the farmhouse is beautiful, of course. At least, it could be.'

To Lucy's concern, she diverted her attention from the road to turn and look at Lucy as she told her, 'He admitted that he hasn't really got much idea what he wants to do with it... It has masses of potential, but it'll take a lot of work. I told him how marvellous you are—'

'Verity, the road,' Lucy interrupted her.

'What? Oh, yes. Well, as I was saying, I told

Niall what marvellous ideas you had and how much you'd helped me when Don and I moved…'

Lucy said nothing. As far as she could recall, she had done nothing other than occasionally accompany Verity on a few of her many sorties into various antique and fabric shops.

'The whole place desperately needs a woman's touch,' Verity continued.

'Well, no doubt it will soon be getting one,' Lucy interrupted her, wanting to change the subject.

Verity looked at her.

'What…has he asked you—?'

'He has a *girlfriend*…remember?' Lucy interrupted her firmly.

'Oh, yes…of course…I'd forgotten for the moment. I saw her photograph, by the way. She's dark…younger than I'd expected. Her name's Beth.'

Beth. It sounded soft and vulnerable, conjuring up for Lucy an immediate mental picture of a girl rather than a woman; someone who was sweetly pretty and rather defenceless, not the kind of partner she would have expected Niall Cameron to choose at all.

'Niall wasn't very forthcoming about her,' Verity added, and Lucy judged from the tone of her voice that she had been disappointed in the amount of information she had managed to extract from him.

'It seems she works in advertising and that she's still on secondment with her company in New York. He didn't say when she was coming back. One thing I did manage to find out, though, and that was that he bought the farmhouse without consulting her.'

'You don't say,' Lucy commented without surprise.

Verity gave her a questioning look.

'You aren't *still* upset about what happened at the dinner party, are you?' she asked her uncertainly. 'I thought that was all sorted out.'

'I'm not upset at all,' Lucy assured her crisply. 'I just don't happen to like the man.'

For once Verity seemed unable to think of anything to say.

Lucy knew her friend meant well, but she cringed to think of how open to misinterpretation Verity's comments about her supposed interior-design skills could have been to Niall Cameron.

Verity was one of those women who could not believe that her single female friends were quite content with their single state, and there had been other occasions in the past when she had tried to matchmake on Lucy's behalf. Then Lucy had merely been wryly amused; this time it was different.

Fortunately the prospect of buying new clothes

superseded the subject of Niall Cameron, and for the rest of the afternoon Verity's conversation was mercifully free of any mention of him.

It was pointless denying to herself that there were sometimes occasions when she came close to mildly envying Verity her self-indulgent approach to life, Lucy reflected when they headed back to the car, Verity carrying several expensive, shiny carrier-bags containing her purchases, which included not only the new dress, but a suit as well, plus a pair of shoes and a new handbag.

They were over halfway back when Verity announced, 'We aren't far from the farm. We could make a detour and call in, if you like. I know that Niall will be there, and—'

'No,' Lucy interrupted her firmly, fiercely controlling the panicky beat of her heart and the way her pulse had suddenly started to race.

The last person she wanted to see was Niall Cameron, the last place she wanted to be his home. She tried not to visualise the photograph of his girlfriend that Verity had described to her.

Why did he keep tormenting her like this? she wondered frantically. *Why* did he keep infiltrating her thoughts, disturbing her peace of mind, obsessing her almost?

Once the repairs to the cottage were done and she was free of her burden of guilt and responsibility, *then* she would be free of him, she told herself, seizing gratefully on this comforting reassurance that what she was enduring was merely some temporary aberration which would soon, hopefully, be over.

CHAPTER FIVE

THE letter came the following Saturday morning.

Lucy had had a busy week at work, staying late several evenings, and she had been looking forward to a quiet weekend, and now this.

She had picked it up without any premonition of what it held, merely noting absently that it was typed and that it somehow looked official.

Until she opened it she imagined vaguely that it held a communication from the estate agents, but once she had extracted the letter from the envelope and unfolded it both her hands and her brain had gone cold with shock and fear.

She read it quickly once, and then, as her heart started to pound with sick despair, she read it again, as though somehow she might have misunderstood its contents the first time, as though somehow, by reading it again slowly, she might change its contents.

It only contained three paragraphs, but they were enough. They were writing, so the typescript informed her, on behalf of their client Eric Barnes, who was her tenant in the property known as the Cottage, Mallow Lane, Marsh End, Collingdean, and they were giving her formal notice that, unless repairs to the property were put in hand within a period of four weeks from the date of their letter, their client would institute legal proceedings against her, not only for the full cost of the repairs, but also for a substantial sum for damages, legal costs and the health hazard of living in the property in its present state.

Lucy tried to read the letter again, but she couldn't because her hand was trembling too much for her to be able to focus on the typescript.

There seemed to be a painful constriction in her chest, making it difficult for her to breathe. She felt sick and dizzy, still half unable to credit what she had read.

Why now...why now, when she was doing all she could to get the work done, and she had told Eric Barnes that? And then abruptly she remembered Niall Cameron asking her when she would have the work done. She wasn't sure yet, she had told him. It could be several months, he had suggested, and she had agreed.

He had *known...known* that when this letter had been written. He had known that there was no way the work could be started within the four weeks' time limit stipulated.

Tears blurred her eyes. She had no doubts at all that *he* was behind the letter, that *he* was the one who had decided on that time limit, knowing that she could not possibly meet it. What did he *want* from her? she wondered bitterly. Blood?

Did *he* share his uncle's obvious belief that she had wealth, money, which she was cold-bloodedly refusing to use to effect the repairs? Was *that* the reason for this letter? Did he think she was *deliberately* lying, *deliberately* trying to evade her responsibilities?

Panic clawed at her as she was forced to contemplate the outcome of a court case against her. There was no doubt about her legal responsibility, she knew that, but to be forced to pay the crippling costs of a legal action and compensation... She trembled violently. She *had* to sit down...to think...to find some way out of this terrifying nightmare.

At lunchtime, after two hours sitting poring over various columns of figures, she pressed her hands to her aching temples and acknowledged that there was no way it could be done.

Even if she sold the flat today, and her furniture as well...even if she found a builder who could start work virtually immediately, there was simply no way she could meet that four-week time limit.

She stood up shakily and wondered wildly if she

could persuade the bank to advance the money against the sale of her flat, and then acknowledged that she could not take that kind of risk. If it did not sell quickly she would be faced with the additional burden of high interest payments to meet as well as everything else.

No, she acknowledged sickly, there was only one thing she could do now.

She dressed carefully, a neat dark navy suit, her best, in fact, one she normally only wore when she was seeing clients, a soft cream silk shirt, toning navy tights, and polished navy shoes.

She checked her appearance in her full-length mirror. She had washed her hair and it swung neatly against her shoulders. Did her make-up cover the dark shadows under her eyes and hide the panic that filled her? Did she look cool, composed, business-like...a woman in control of herself and her life? It was important that she presented the right image; that she looked confident; that she did not betray the terror she could feel inside her.

She drove there slowly and carefully. She should perhaps have rung first, but supposing he had refused to see her? He *must* know, of course, that she would get in touch with him, and no doubt he would have enjoyed drawing out her torment, refusing to see her...making her wait. Well, this way *she* had taken the initiative...had shown, would show him, that she was not so easily intimidated as he supposed.

She knew the way to the farmhouse, of course. The Discovery was parked on the cobbled yard. She had to get out of her car to open the farm gate that led to it. Even though the weather had been dry for the last week, the lane was still muddy. She had come prepared, though. Grimly she pulled on her old trainers and got out of her car to open the gate so that she could drive through and park behind the Discovery.

Once she had done so, once the gate was secured, she changed her trainers for her court shoes, carefully removing the mud on her fingers with a damp wipe.

Her heart was hammering against her ribs. She could feel her face starting to burn with tension and anxiety. She had never felt more afraid or more alone in her life, but she kept her head held high as she marched up to the front door and rapped firmly on the worn metal knocker.

It seemed a long time before Niall came to the door, and when he did open it it was obvious that he must have been outside in the garden, because he was wearing a pair of thick socks over the bottoms of his jeans, the kind one wore inside wellingtons.

'So it *is* you.' He was frowning at her. 'I thought I recognised your car.'

He was an excellent actor, Lucy admitted. From the look on his face, she might almost have supposed that she were the last person he had expected to find on his doorstep, when he must have known that that letter would bring her here.

She didn't waste any time. She was determined that if she had to beg then at least she would do so with pride. She would not allow him to make her crawl or grovel.

'I think we have something to discuss,' she told him coldly.

His frown deepened.

'Do we?' he asked unhelpfully.

Lucy was determined not to let him get the better of her, or to intimidate her.

'I'm sorry if it spoils your fun,' she told him curtly. 'But I have no intention of playing games. The letter arrived this morning.'

'The letter? What letter? Look, you'd better come in,' he told her, standing back from the door so that she could step inside.

Tensely she did so. The doorway was only narrow, and, slight though she was, she had to press her spine against the door-jamb to keep as much distance between their bodies as she could. Even so, she could still smell the earthy male scent of his skin and, although she didn't even look at him, she had a brief, reckless mental image of him working in the garden, beads of sweat dampening his skin, darkening the V of hair she could see in the opening of his cotton shirt.

Now her tension was not only caused by her anxiety and misery over the contents of the solicitor's letter folded in her handbag.

The hallway was cool and dark after the warm sunshine outside. The farmhouse was old; it smelled faintly of lavender, wax polish and old wood, not an unpleasant smell and one which evoked images of a warm family home, of the bustle and the busyness of a practical farmer's wife, raising a large brood of children and running a comfortable, happy home.

That was her weakness, Lucy decided, that she could never quite shake off this need in her to escape into some fantasy world of happy families.

Deriding herself for it, she tried to quieten her uneasy nerves.

'This way,' Niall directed her.

He had moved quietly over the stone-flagged floor. Those socks, of course, and now he was standing almost directly behind her. It was quite impossible that she should actually be able to feel any heat coming off his body, she told herself, but even so she still instinctively moved away from him, unwilling to acknowledge that, while mentally she thoroughly disliked him, on a deeper and far more primitive level she was unwelcomely aware of him as a man.

He was the kind of man who would enjoy that type of knowledge, she told herself bitterly, just as he had enjoyed the punishment of that angry kiss.

She stayed where she was while he opened one of the doors off the hallway and then waited for her to walk into the room.

Sunlight cast oblongs of mellow light through the leaded windows. The room ran the full width of the house, with windows at either end and a window-seat that overlooked the rear garden. The room was sparsely, but not unattractively furnished, although Lucy knew that the faded old brocades of the chairs and the sofa would not have appealed to Verity's taste for bright, modern glazed chintzes with ribbons and bows.

Lucy, though, liked it, her fingers itching to touch the soft, worn fabric; she realised with a small pang that, while she rarely if ever spontaneously touched another human being, she must subconsciously be suppressing a very deep-seated need because she often found herself touching things, furniture, fabric, china, as though this was her only outlet for the tactile side of her nature.

A small *frisson* of anxiety touched her skin, and,

although she could have sworn she controlled it instantly, Niall must have seen it because he asked immediately if she was cold.

She shook her head. Her fingers might be icy with tension and fright, but inwardly she was burning with panic and despair.

'Verity tells me the house lacks a woman's touch,' he commented, startling her so much that she actually looked directly at him.

It was a mistake. His mouth suddenly had a humorous curve to it, a warmth that she didn't want to recognise.

'Furnishing a home is a very individual thing,' Lucy responded. Her throat felt tight and sore. What on earth was she doing, making small talk with him, when all she wanted to do was to get the purpose of her visit over with?

'Mm. And something which, generally speaking, women are better at than men. It's a feminine rather than a masculine instinct to clothe starkness in softness and comfort, I suspect.'

Lucy looked at the photograph on one of the tables. This must be his girlfriend. She recognised her from Verity's description. Yes, she was the sort of woman—or girl, rather—who would make a man think of her as being soft and feminine.

'Beth hasn't seen the house yet.'

Lucy flushed as she realised that Niall had seen her studying the photograph.

'I'm not sure that she'll like it.'

He shrugged as though he found the thought unimportant, and Lucy felt a renewed spark of dislike. What kind of man was he not to care whether or not his lover had any say, any choice in their shared home? However, it was hardly any business of hers. She was here for a different purpose entirely.

She opened her handbag and removed the letter.

'I wanted to discuss this with you,' she told him curtly, her control breaking a little, emotion darkening her eyes as she challenged, 'You must know that I can't possibly meet the terms it sets out…a time limit of four weeks. It's impossible.'

She could hear her voice starting to tremble as the panic overwhelmed her. She swallowed hard and stopped speaking. She must not lose control; she must keep calm. She must not abase herself completely.

She could see that he was frowning. Waiting for her to start pleading with him, she guessed. The knot of pain in her stomach had become an agonising, heavy weight.

'I have promised to get the work done just as soon as I can, and I intend to keep that promise. This letter—'

'May I see it?'

He reached out, taking the letter from her before she could stop him.

Now it was her turn to frown. Why did he want to *see* it? He must know its contents, after all.

He was reading it, she saw, and while he did his frown was deepening.

Once he had finished he did not hand it back to her. Instead he folded it up and demanded curtly, 'What makes you think the letter was from me? It states plainly enough that the solicitors are acting for my uncle.'

For a moment Lucy was nonplussed. This was something that she had not expected. She had anticipated that he would take pleasure in acknowledging that the decision to go to law had been his. After all, *he* had been the one who had pointed out that possibility to her, and until his arrival on the scene Eric Barnes had been content merely to complain verbally about the state of the cottage.

'*You* were the one who pointed out my legal obligations to me,' she reminded him tensely. 'Naturally, I assumed—'

'That, not content with pointing them out, I would also take steps to have them formally brought to your notice?' he suggested drily.

'Mr Barnes…your uncle had never even mentioned taking any kind of legal action, much less suing me for damages, until you arrived here,' she told him hotly, suddenly feeling as though she was guilty of some kind of biased and unfair misjudgement.

'I pointed out the possibility, yes,' he agreed quietly. 'But I am certainly not responsible for this.' He put the letter down on a small table at his side. 'When you said that you intended to have the repairs carried out I assumed that the problem was over.'

Lucy stared at him, confusion and doubt shadowing her eyes. She felt dizzy…faint… uncomfortably weak; her legs, she discovered, were trembling.

'But—'

'I think you should sit down,' she heard Niall Cameron saying to her, but the words seemed to reach her down a long dark tunnel. She heard a muffled sound, a curse, it seemed, and then she was pitching forward into a frightening whirlpool of darkness.

She heard herself cry out as she fainted, a thin, sharp sound of fear, and then thankfully the fall ended, although the darkness still continued to engulf her.

She came round almost immediately, her brain so clumsy that it took several seconds after her consciousness had started to return before she realised that the solid, comfortable substance against which she was leaning was Niall Cameron's body, and that the soothing steady sound she could hear was his heartbeat. Once she did realise she panicked and struggled to push herself away from him, but his arms, she realised, were wrapped around her.

'It's all right,' she heard him saying softly. 'You fainted. Hardly surprising, really,' she heard him adding, increasing her confusion. There was a note of grim anger in his voice that made her wince, her body flinching as she recognised her own inability to defend herself from that anger. 'I suppose you've been worrying yourself half to death since you got it.'

He still sounded angry, his voice at odds with his oddly sympathetic words.

It was all part of his plan to undermine her, to humiliate her, she decided hazily.

'I wasn't lying about having the work done,' she told him fiercely. He was holding her so tightly that she couldn't push herself away from his body enough to look directly into his face. It was an extremely disturbing sensation, feeling the warmth of her own breath bouncing back at her from the exposed V of flesh at his throat.

'But I can't guarantee to have it started within four weeks.'

'No, you can't, can you?' he agreed grimly.

Her heart sank. So he had simply been tormenting her, playing with her, mocking her in allowing her to think he was expressing sympathy. She was starting to feel very weak and sick, a physical re-action to all the emotional stress she had been suf-fering.

'Please, let me go,' she demanded shakily.

'What, and risk having you faint on me again? When was the last time you ate properly?' he de-manded, further shocking her.

She stiffened in his arms. What was he…an expert in verbal torture, one moment cold and taunt-ing, the next…?

'When and what I eat is none of your business,' she told him frostily.

'It is when you pass out in front of me,' he con-tradicted flatly. 'What's wrong? Can't you afford a decent meal?'

The taunt made her gasp in outrage.

'Of course I can,' she denied. 'I eat as much as I need.'

'So how come you've lost so much weight? And don't try telling me you're on a diet,' he derided her.

Lucy was angry now.

'What makes you think I have lost weight?' she demanded. She was still trying to put some distance between them, and abruptly he loosened his hold a little so that she stumbled back against the hard constraint of his imprisoning forearm as she looked bitterly up at him.

'I don't *think*. I *know*,' he told her shortly. 'I've got eyes in my head, and, even if I couldn't see, I can feel how much thinner you are.'

Her shock showed in her eyes, a burning wave of mingled embarrassment and awareness staining her skin.

He had barely touched her that night...barely held her for any length of time. Was he really trying to imply that he could remember how she had felt well enough to compare the difference in her body?

His words conjured up an intimacy that made her confused and afraid. It was as though in some way he knew more about her body than she did herself; that he had a knowledge of it that was denied to her.

'Why didn't you *tell* me that the only way you could raise the money to repair the cottage was by selling your own home?'

Now he *had* shocked her. He was looking directly into her eyes so that there was no way she could shield herself from him.

'Why should I?' she demanded. 'How I raise the money isn't any concern of yours...or anyone else's.' She bit her lip, trembling suddenly. 'How did you know?' she asked him huskily. 'About my selling the flat, I mean? No one knows yet. The agent hasn't even advertised it.'

'I didn't know,' he told her grimly. 'I guessed.'

Now her humiliation was totally complete, and it made her lash out at him verbally, driven by the pain tearing into her.

'Really? I thought you shared my uncle's view that I was a woman of considerable wealth, that I was refusing to have the repairs done out of greed and selfishness.' She stopped abruptly as she heard the rising note of hysteria in her own voice.

'Originally, yes. I thought that there was some question of your deliberately refusing to have the work done for—shall we say?—less than altruistic motives, but after I'd made one or two enquiries—'

Lucy's gasp of outrage silenced him.

'You made enquiries about *me*?' she demanded huskily. 'From whom? My friends...? What did you do? Ask them to give you a list of my known assets? How do you know that they know the truth? How do you know that I'm not lying to them, as you obviously thought I was to your uncle?'

'Stop it,' he said kindly, shaking her gently, as though she were a hysterical child and not an adult woman, she recognised numbly.

'Look, I know you've had a bad shock. Come and sit down. I'll make some tea and then we'll discuss this whole thing rationally.'

She wanted to protest that the last thing she wanted was to hold any kind of conversation, rational or otherwise, with him, but somehow she found herself being led over to the deep-cushioned settee and gently pushed down on to it.

It was odd how much she missed the comforting warmth of his body, she recognised dully when he had left her to go and make the tea.

Comforting. Warm. Niall Cameron. The man who had virtually accused her of deceit. Was she going mad?

What was she doing here, anyway? Why didn't she simply get up and leave? It was obvious now that there was no point in discussing the contents of the letter with Niall, no point in asking him to give her more time if he was not its instigator.

She was halfway out of her seat when he came back with the tea.

Uncomfortably she sat down again. He had, she saw, set the tray with china cups, and there were thin slices of lemon as well as milk.

'My grandmother brought us up and she was a stickler for the correct procedure.'

'Us?' Lucy queried uncertainly.

'Me and my sister. Our mother died in a car accident that left my father semi-paralysed, so my grandmother brought us up and looked after my father.'

He had poured her tea, and he offered her milk or lemon before he handed it to her.

'Milk, please,' she told him.

What was he going to say to her? What could he say to her? she wondered nervously as she sipped her tea.

If, as he had intimated, the decision to take legal action against her was his uncle's then what was there that he could do?

His cool, 'I have a proposition to put to you,' made her tense, the tea slopping against the sides of her cup slightly.

She put it down, trying to look calm and in control, her eyes wary as they met his.

'What kind of proposition?' she asked him.

'I want to buy the cottage,' he told her.

She stared at him in disbelief.

'You want to *buy* it? But—'

'Of course, you'll want to have it valued professionally. I don't know what that valuation will be.'

'It's a liability, not an asset,' Lucy told him, too stunned to prevaricate. 'It isn't worth anything.'

The way he looked at her made her skin burn, for no apparent reason other than the fact that he was looking at her.

'I can't let you buy it,' she told him in a muffled voice. 'You *know* it isn't worth anything.'

'Not to anyone else, perhaps, but to me it is,' he

contradicted her. 'After all, it is my uncle's home. And it seems that it's also the only home that he's willing to accept. It also seems to me that for me to buy it would solve all our problems.'

It would certainly solve hers, Lucy admitted, but why should he want to do such a thing when they both knew that she was legally obliged to repair the place? Once she sold it to him that responsibility would pass to him.

Something of what she was feeling must have registered on her face, because he put down his own teacup and turned away from her, almost as though he didn't want her to see his face as he told her briefly, 'This area is my home now. Unlike my uncle, I have no wish to isolate myself from the rest of the human race. And, besides, there is Beth to consider. When she comes back she won't want to find that almost the entire local community won't have anything to do with us because I am partially responsible for forcing you to give up your home.'

'No one would think that,' Lucy protested.

He turned round then, giving her an extremely sardonic look.

'If you really believe that you are indeed naïve. Surely you realise the affection in which you are held...how protective people feel towards you? The shy, protected seventeen-year-old, suddenly or-

phaned, so proud and so vulnerable that she made
everyone else's heart ache in sympathy for her.'

Lucy went white.

'Who told you that?' she demanded wildly.

'No one…in those exact words, but it wasn't
hard to read between the lines.'

'I don't want your pity,' Lucy told him stiffly.

She couldn't look at him, but the silence
stretched on for so long that eventually she had to.

'No, I don't expect you do,' he agreed drily. 'In
fact, I suspect that you don't want anything from
me at all, do you, Lucy? That you'd rather lose your
home than accept what is, after all, a perfectly valid
and reasonable suggestion from me; that I buy from
you the place that is my uncle's home. Or isn't it
pride that makes you refuse? Is it perhaps that my
uncle was right when he claimed that you want him
out of the cottage?'

'No,' Lucy denied vehemently, and as she saw
the satisfaction in his eyes she knew that she had
fallen into a cleverly baited trap.

'Good. Then you will give my offer serious consideration, won't you?' he pressed softly.

His voice might be soft, but Lucy was under no
illusions. She knew that he intended to have his
own way.

She got up shakily, leaving her half-finished tea.

'I'll give it consideration,' she agreed gravely.

He accompanied her to her car, and then, just as she was unlocking the door, he stopped her, putting his hand on her arm.

The warmth of that touch, the power she could feel in its steady, deceptively gentle constraint, shocked through her whole body.

'Oh, and Lucy.'

She looked tensely at him.

'Make sure you have something to eat,' he told her. 'You can't afford to lose any more weight.'

'Why...because men don't like thin women?' she challenged, and instantly she knew it was the wrong thing to say.

'Is that why you do it?' he asked her, watching her. 'Oh, yes, I've heard about that too,' he told her. 'What is it that makes you hold my sex so determinedly at a distance, Lucy? Fear?'

'No,' she denied angrily.

He smiled at her then, a smile that sent her pulse-rate soaring and which made her heart crash frantically against the cage of her ribs.

'Good.'

'GOOD.' What exactly did that mean? Lucy wondered fiercely as she drove home. What could it possibly mean when he was already involved with someone else, and she...well, she didn't like him, anyway, did she?

CHAPTER SIX

LUCY opened her eyes and glanced sleepily at her alarm clock.

Ten o'clock! It couldn't possibly be. She *never* slept that long. She was *always* up early. She blinked and studied the clock again. It *was* definitely ten o'clock, and she had slept so deeply that she had barely disturbed the covers.

What was she supposed to read into that? she wondered uneasily as she stretched luxuriously beneath the duvet and then pushed it back so that she could get up.

Relief because Niall Cameron had offered her a way out of her problems, and a way out, moreover, which would enable her to keep her home?

Why was he doing it? Not for her. Why should he? For his uncle, then...or perhaps for Beth. From her photograph, she did not look the type who would easily be able to deal with someone like Eric Barnes, and, although Niall had said nothing yesterday, she suspected that he was shrewd enough to have got his uncle's measure and to have recognised that he was the kind of person who enjoyed causing problems, who liked being contrary.

Had he always been like that, or was it simply something that had come with old age and loneliness, a way of rejecting a world that he might have felt had also rejected him? People who lived lonely, isolated lives did tend to develop odd beliefs, odd fixations. Would *she* become like that?

She stood still, dismayed by the prospect, quickly dismissing it.

Once she was up an unfamiliar restlessness possessed her, a desire to step outside her familiar routine. She was getting far too set in her ways, she acknowledged. A tiny shiver of alarm touched her spine.

Just because she liked her life to follow a certain orderly pattern it did not mean she was going to turn into an eccentric recluse, she told herself firmly. There was nothing wrong in having order and pattern to one's life...except when that order become so important that its importance superseded everything else, leaving no room and certainly no desire for anything that was different, spontaneous!

She was letting her imagination run away with her, she told herself as she pulled on her running shoes.

There was no sun this morning, and outside it was correspondingly cool.

She warmed up with a slow jog and then let her body slip into the easy familiar pace at which she ran. It crossed her mind as she did so that in her running, as in everything else in her life, she needed to be the one in control, the pace never so demanding that it was allowed to dominate her.

She shook the thought away. She did not want to have to deal with such deep and disturbing thoughts; one of her aims in this weekly ritual was to relieve her body of any mental stress, not to add to it, and yet at the same time as the thought formed she had a brief mental image of Niall Cameron. Immediately she started to increase her pace, to run just that bit faster, pushing her body that little bit harder—so that it wouldn't be able to torment her with the self-indulgence of thinking about him?

Why should thinking about Niall Cameron bother her? She could feel the strain in her muscles now, the fierce pound of her heart, the sweat dampening her skin. All right, so physically there was something about him—some innate subtle masculinity that appealed subconsciously and subversively to her senses—so what did that mean? Nothing…nothing at all, other than that she was in some vague way physically responsive to him.

Some *vague* way. Her heartbeat accelerated abruptly, its unsteady thud nothing to do with her physical exercise.

Even if they had not been on opposite sides over the problem of her cottage and his uncle, even if she had been foolish enough to read into his attitude towards her some stray suggestion that he found her attractive and desirable, *he* was committed to someone else.

But they weren't on opposite sides any longer, were they, not since he had made that extraordinary offer to buy the cottage from her? And as for being attracted to her...

But he *was* committed to someone else. To Beth. Saying her name, conjuring up from her memory her photograph, reminded Lucy very firmly of just how strong and real that commitment was.

But why should she need reminding?

She collected her papers, paid for them, firmly ignoring the admiring glance a fellow customer was giving her, jogged for a couple of hundred yards to cool down, and then walked briskly the rest of the way home.

As she walked down the drive to her apartment the first thing she saw was Niall's Discovery. Which was odd, really, in view of its discreet colour and the fact that it was parked very neatly and unobtrusively with several other far more striking vehicles, but *she* had still seen it immediately. Seen it and reacted to the sight of it, just as her body was now reacting to the sight of its owner walking easily towards her.

Her heart was thumping at least twice as fast as it should have been, her breath coming in sharp, difficult gasps, her body suddenly drenched with heat, while her muscles quivered with shock, all symptoms that could have been put down to her exercise, but which she knew quite well were caused exclusively by the man coming towards her, smiling at her.

'I've been up to your door. When I realised you weren't in I thought I'd wait to see if you came back. I knew you couldn't have gone far. Your car's still here.'

She was trembling physically now, and she realised that Niall was aware of it as well when he suddenly stopped speaking to study her.

'It's no wonder you're losing weight,' he told her, frowning at her. 'You should never force your body beyond its own limits of physical endurance.'

Did he think she was a complete fool? Lucy wondered irritably. He was dressed in a pair of well-washed faded clean jeans, a comfortably soft blue work-shirt tucked into their waistband. He looked cool and relaxed, making her uncomfortably conscious of her own sticky, untidy appearance. Her hair was starting to escape from its plait, and wisps of it were clinging damply to her face. Her shorts and top were soaked with perspiration, and now that she had stopped running her skin felt uncomfortably clammy. She was, she discovered, even starting to shiver a little.

Niall saw it too. His eyebrows came together in a quick frown.

'You're cold,' he told her.

The man was impossible. Did he think she needed *him* to tell her that?

'Yes,' she agreed, side-stepping him, giving him as wide a berth as she possibly could, unwilling to admit even to herself the reason she was so anxious to keep a distance between them.

'I came round to see if you'd reached any decision about selling the cottage to me,' he told her.

Lucy had been walking towards the building. Now she stopped.

'I thought we could discuss the whole thing over lunch,' Niall continued, apparently unaware of her tension.

'Lunch?' Lucy glanced at her watch and realised that her late start meant that it was now almost twelve o'clock.

'I...I can't,' she told him, panic seizing her. 'I have to shower...wash my hair...'

'That's all right, he responded easily. 'I can wait.'

Outmanoeuvred, Lucy worried at her bottom lip.

Why on earth hadn't she simply told him that she didn't *want* to have lunch with him, instead of trying to make some feeble excuse?

Was the man really as thick-skinned as he seemed? Couldn't he *see* how reluctant she was to spend time with him? Didn't he realise?

Didn't he realise what? she asked herself bitterly. Didn't he realise how dangerously attractive she found him? Did she *want* him to realise that? Did she *want* to add that ultimate humiliation to all the other small humiliations she seemed to have endured at his hands?

And what was she so afraid of... what could she say to him—'I can't have lunch with you because I don't trust you... because I don't trust myself'? Hardly!

When she walked into the building and towards her front door he was right beside her.

'Here, let me take those,' he offered, relieving her of the newspapers she had been about to put on the floor while she fished the chain she wore around her neck out of her top.

Her keys were on it, a small precaution she took whenever she went running, not trusting herself not to lose the keys from her shorts's pocket.

Her top was still damp and the keys had become lodged in the front of her bra somehow, and as she tugged irritably at the chain perhaps a little too roughly it snapped.

Niall was, she recognised, watching her. The keys were now firmly lodged in the front of her bra, and the only way she was going to be able to remove them was to pull up the waistband of her top and fish them out.

Her skin felt unpleasantly warm, tiny prickles of perspiration dampening it, a tight and not exactly unpleasant sensation gathering in the pit of her stomach.

Ignoring it, she firmly turned her back on Niall; her fingers felt clumsy, taking a ridiculous amount of time to obey her instructions to lift up her top.

The trouble was that the fabric was now damp and clinging to her skin, rubbing a little uncomfortably against it as she tugged at it.

Niall couldn't see anything, of course. She had her back to him, but at the same time she was stupidly conscious of the fact that he was there.

As she gave the top a quick, angry yank she felt the coolness of fresh air against the sticky skin of her midriff and her back. Her spine tensed, a fierce spiral of relief twisting through her as her hand closed over the keys.

Trying to control the way she was shaking, she pulled down her top and unlocked the front door, but once they were inside her small hallway it was Niall who put the safety chain across the lock.

'A woman on her own can't be too careful,' he told her quietly as she watched.

Lucy ignored him; her plait was a heavy, uncomfortable weight on the back of her neck. It felt as though it had almost disintegrated. She pushed nervous fingers against her nape, grimacing as she felt the moistness of her skin.

All she wanted to do was strip off and enjoy the cool, cleansing freshness of her shower, but she could hardly just leave Niall waiting for her.

She ought at least to offer him a cup of coffee.

She did so, tensing at the way he suddenly smiled at her.

'What is it you find so amusing?' she demanded, for once ignoring the cautionary voice inside her that would normally have quelled the voicing of such a question.

'You,' he told her softly, adding, 'Trying to suppress all that anger and irritation; trying to be the well-mannered, well-brought-up woman your parents so obviously taught you to be. We're in the nineties now, Lucy,' he told her drily. 'People *are* allowed to express their emotions; didn't you know?'

Lucy was dumbfounded. An enormous wave of irritation and helpless anger rolled over her. If she

expressed hers he would not be standing in her hallway right now, but, even though he was watching
her, her training went too deep, and she couldn't
express what she was feeling.

Giving way to one's emotions was dangerous because once they had escaped it might be impossible
ever to regain control of them again. She could remember vividly how close to losing her control she
had come when her parents had died, and how
frightened, how terrified she had been. Even thinking about it now made her stomach muscles curl in
protest.

'I'll just make some coffee,' she told him frig-
idly.

As she turned away from him she wondered if
the look she had surprised in his eyes could actually
have been disappointment. Had he *wanted* her to
give way to her temper, to tell him to go? Had he
been looking to her to put a stop now to something
which they both knew…?

She mercilessly sliced off the thought, as though
by not allowing it to form, not allowing herself to
think, she was somehow safeguarding herself from
some kind of danger.

She was just about to open the kitchen door when
she heard Niall saying quietly, 'Hang on a second.'

She stopped automatically, giving him a brief
questioning look over her shoulder as he caught up

with her, but when she felt the cool pressure of his hand against the small of her back, pulling down her top to cover the skin she had inadvertently left bare, her surprise turned to sharp tension.

As she pulled away from him and he stopped her she realised that there was nowhere for her to go. The kitchen door was closed and he was right behind her.

'It's all right,' he told her calmly. 'It's just that your top was all rucked up. You shouldn't let your body get cold after you've been exercising. That's how muscles get damaged and how rheumatism sets in.'

He was still standing behind her. Lucy felt as though she dared not move, as though she dared not breathe almost. There had been nothing remotely sexual in his touch, she recognised now that her body was recovering from its initial panic, but then just as she had started to relax she felt his fingers drift against the nape of her neck, pushing gently at the strands of hair that covered it.

'What is it, I wonder, about the nape of a woman's neck that is both so vulnerable and somehow so enticingly sensual?'

His thumb was rubbing gently at her skin, causing a starburst of sensation to explode through her body, producing a rash of goose-bumps which he couldn't avoid noticing. At the same time she could almost feel her breasts swelling, and she could certainly feel and see the taut, excited way her nipples had hardened.

'Your skin feels like velvet. Did you know that one of the most erotic scents there is to a man is the warm womanly smell of a healthily exercised body?'

Lucy jerked frantically away from him, her sharp, 'Don't,' ricocheting off the walls of the enclosed space.

As she pulled open the kitchen door she was too afraid to look at him.

She could hear him moving around the room behind her, but she ignored him, grimly setting about making them both some coffee.

He hadn't meant anything personal by his comment, she told herself fiercely. He couldn't have done. They were obviously two people with completely opposing ways of living. She could never, ever imagine herself making that kind of remark with his casual insouciance. To her it was the kind of comment exchanged only by the most intimate of lovers, and, even though she was probably even more acutely aware of the scent of his skin, of its texture, its maleness and of the very dangerous excitement that that knowledge churned inside her, the very last thing she would ever do would be to comment openly to him on how erotic her senses found him.

Because her awareness of that eroticism was focused on *him*, she suddenly realised with sharp clarity, while his embraced all her sex. His comment had been impersonal, casual, the passing awareness of certain aspects of her sexuality which he, as a male, appreciated, but which meant nothing more personal to him than that, while she...

The coffee was ready. She poured it into two mugs, put his on a tray, together with some wholemeal biscuits, and carried the tray through into her sitting-room, all without saying a word to him.

She put the tray down and turned to him. Niall was studying a photograph of her parents.

'You obviously loved them a great deal.'

There he went again, saying things that should not be said, watching her with eyes that saw far too much.

'Yes,' she agreed tersely.

He was looking at her now, and she was suddenly aware of the briefness of her shorts, of the way the soft, fine cotton-knit fabric clung to her body, and yet there was nothing prurient or distasteful about the way he was watching her. She had no fear, for instance, that he was about to touch her...attack her. No, her fears sprang from her own awareness of the effect he had on her, on the way her breasts now felt oddly heavy, unfamiliarly tender.

'I'll go and have my shower,' she told him quickly. 'I shan't be long.'

Her heart was thumping frantically as she hurried into her bedroom.

Lunch, he had said…and it was a business lunch, that was all, she reminded herself sternly. Just because it was Sunday…just because he was standing in her sitting-room, dressed in those casual jeans that clung so softly to his body…

Lunch, she reminded herself feverishly. He couldn't be intending to take her anywhere formal, that was obvious from his clothes, so what should she wear, then? Something that showed she acknowledged that it was a business lunch; that they were together simply to discuss the sale of her cottage. Something that discreetly declared the formality of their purely business association.

Her fingers trembled tensely as she rifled through her clothes, eventually extracting a taupe-coloured suit and the taupe and navy top that went with it.

A little bit over-formal perhaps, given his jeans and casual shirt, but there was no harm in letting him know just how she viewed their relationship, no harm in letting him know that it was strictly business.

And yet ten minutes later, standing under the

shower, quickly soaping her body as her hand inadvertently brushed against an erect nipple, she was immediately reminded of the feeling that had overpowered her when he had touched the nape of her neck.

She closed her eyes, her body outwardly motionless but inwardly filled with the most intense and dangerous sensual messages and feelings. Her body quivered, a deep-seated, powerful convulsion of sensation gripping her, her skin suddenly so sensitive that she had to fight against imagining the touch of his hands against it, the touch of his mouth.

Trembling violently, she turned the cold tap on as hard as she could, gasping as the shock of the icy water hit her skin.

Stepping out of the shower, she dried herself quickly, almost roughly, as though punishing her body for its obstinate refusal to accept that it must not respond to Niall Cameron with such feverish intensity.

Once she was dressed, clothed in her suit, and in the persona of her formal business self, she felt a little better. She had replaited her wet hair, and the severity of the style suited her mood. Having applied her usual discreet make-up and had a quick check that she looked cool and withdrawn, and most definitely not the kind of woman a man would feel inclined to reach out for either physically or emotionally, she went back to the sitting-room.

Niall stood up as she arrived. His glance flicked discreetly over her, and, if he was contrasting the casualness of his own attire with the formality of hers, he made no comment about it.

'I like this room,' he told her easily. 'Verity told me that you had a very good eye for design and colour, and that you had a flair for turning a house into a home. I can see now what she means.'

'This room wasn't designed,' Lucy denied, instantly retreating from his compliment. 'Most of the things in here came from my parents' house.'

The second comment she made more reluctantly, suddenly aware of how much it might reveal about her; things she might not want to reveal, especially to this particular man.

'Yes,' he agreed softly.

Lucy shot him a wary, defensive look, wondering exactly what lay behind the thoughtful, almost sad look he was giving her.

'You look very like your mother.'

Lucy blinked quickly. It was true that she did, but people so rarely commented on that likeness that Niall's doing so made her feel vulnerable.

'Children do often resemble their parents,' she pointed out tersely, rejecting his comment almost, as she was trying to reject her awareness of him, her realisation that here was a man who she could have...

Could have what? Loved? What a ridiculous notion. Until yesterday they had been enemies. She knew nothing about him. Other than the fact that when he touched her her whole body became physically attuned to him, aroused by him; other than the fact that when she was with him she felt so vibrantly alive. Other than the fact that he was committed to another woman and that that commitment meant, to her at least, that there could be no kind of emotional or physical relationship between them.

Perhaps that was *why* she was so drawn to him, she decided. Because she knew that he was out of bounds.

'You still miss your parents very much, don't you?'

Niall's soft question came as a shock. These days so few people mentioned her parents. After all, their deaths had occurred almost a decade ago.

Instead of answering him honestly, she tensed and demanded defensively, 'What makes you say that?'

She didn't like the fact that he could so easily interpret her feelings, her thoughts, and certainly didn't like the way he had seen so easily and so clearly what other people closer to her never seemed to realise.

'You surround yourself with tangible memories of them,' he told her quietly. 'So much so that it's almost as though you're afraid of letting go, of being alone.'

'That's rubbish,' she denied quickly, her face suddenly hot, her body tense. 'I'm not afraid of being alone at all.'

He gave her a long, uninterpretable look.

'No. What are you afraid of, then? Intimacy, perhaps?'

Her throat locked as panic swirled through her. She felt as though she had pushed open a door and suddenly found herself in a totally alien and terrifying world.

'I thought you wanted to discuss buying the cottage, not psychoanalysing me,' she snapped as soon as her vocal muscles relaxed enough for her to speak.

'So prickly and defensive,' Niall commented. He had picked up another silver-framed photograph, one of herself as a baby sitting on her mother's lap this time. He wasn't looking at her, and yet she was acutely conscious of him. It took all her mental strength to stop herself from snatching the photograph out of his hands and putting it face down on the table.

He made her feel so vulnerable, so much in dan-

ger, and she couldn't understand why, or was it that
she did not want to acknowledge why?

'I thought we were going out to lunch,' Lucy
reminded him, suddenly desperate to get him out of
her home and equally anxious for him not to know
what she was feeling.

He put down the photograph then, much to her
relief, and smiled at her.

'Hungry?' he asked her. 'Good.'

He moved over to the door, opening it for her.
His manners, she acknowledged, were very good,
not showy, simply a part of him; an awareness of
a certain responsibility, not especially towards her,
but, she suspected, to all those who were physically
weaker than he was himself.

It wasn't until she was seated beside him in the
Discovery that she realised that she could quite easily have suggested that they travel in her car and
that that would have given her at least some kind
of control. This way, of the two of them, she was
very much the dependent partner.

Partner. They were not partners…they were two
strangers, thrown together by an unwanted quirk of
fate. Once all this business of the cottage was resolved there would be no need for her to have any
kind of contact with him.

Except that he was one of Don's clients. Except
that socially there would be occasions when she

would no doubt have to meet him. And Beth. She must not forget Beth.

Think about the cottage, she warned herself. His offer had come so unexpectedly yesterday that she had hardly had time yet to realise what had happened.

She couldn't deny what a relief it would be to be rid of any responsibility for the cottage and for its tenant, but she was still reluctant to accept his offer…to accept his charity, because it had to be charity, didn't it? No one could possibly want to buy that ramshackle, run-down place.

Unless, of course, they happened to have a stubborn old uncle who lived there and refused to live anywhere else.

'I've had a word with Eric about that letter, by the way,' Niall told her, interrupting her train of thought.

'I've explained to him that I'm negotiating to buy the cottage from you, and I've arranged to go with him tomorrow to see his solicitors and to explain the full position to them. In the meantime, you can take it that the contents of their letter can be safely ignored.'

'Thank you.'

The words almost stuck in her throat. She turned her head away from him, her muscles tensing with humiliation. If only she could have told him that

his interference, his charity, wasn't necessary; that
somehow miraculously she had found the money to
effect the repairs herself. Her pride longed for her
to be able to do so, but she had to acknowledge
that in this instance pride was a luxury she simply
could not afford.

She had now, as she had had to do when her
parents had first died, to suppress what she was
feeling, and to remind herself that everything had a
price, and that the price of retaining her home was
the swallowing of her pride and the acknowledge-
ment, if somewhat ungracious, of his intervention
on her behalf.

She tried to direct her thoughts along less de-
structive channels by wondering where he could be
taking her for lunch, running mentally through
those places in the locality where Sunday lunch was
served with the kind of informality that permitted
male diners to appear so casually dressed.

She could only think of one and they were trav-
elling in the opposite direction from that. There
were several local pubs that served bar lunches, of
course.

While she was mentally mulling over all the pos-
sibilities she suddenly realised where they were,
and just as Niall turned off the main road and towards his own house she turned to him and demanded, 'Why have you brought me here?'

He gave her a surprised, innocent look as he pulled through the open gate and on to the cobbled yard, stopping the car.

'To have lunch, of course.'

He was opening the Discovery's door and getting out, her protesting, 'But I thought...' lost to him as he walked round to open the passenger-door for her.

It was far too late now for her to tell him that, had she known they would be having lunch in his home, she would never have accepted his invitation, Lucy realised. At least not without making herself look a complete fool and no doubt without also giving rise to those awkward questions he seemed to deliver so expertly and unashamedly.

She could just imagine him asking why she could not have lunch here with him, and what would she say? It was too intimate?

Her skin burned with shamed heat as she acknowledged the impossibility of making *that* particular response.

As he opened the Discovery's door for her and looked at her high-heeled delicate leather shoes, for a moment she half expected him to reach inside the vehicle and physically lift her out, but to her relief he did not, simply commenting, 'It's just as well I managed to get the yard swept. I'd forgotten what hard physical work pushing a yard brush can be.' He flexed his shoulders ruefully as he spoke, as though the muscles still held traces of that strain, and to her consternation Lucy had a very vivid and disturbing mental vision of him stripped to the waist, his torso bare, sleek with sweat, the muscles bunching beneath the sheen of his skin as he worked.

In fact, the image was so compelling, so engrossing, that she almost lost her balance as she stepped down from the Discovery.

Immediately Niall's hand shot out to steady her. She was glad she was wearing her suit and that the fabric of her jacket prevented his hand from coming into direct contact with her skin. She had had enough experience of the havoc that *that* could cause already.

CHAPTER SEVEN

'I KNOW you like salmon, so I played it safe,' Niall commented as he guided Lucy into the kitchen. 'Here, let me take your jacket.'

'No...no. I prefer to keep it on.'

She tensed as he gave her a brief, almost frowning look.

'You don't feel cold, do you?' he questioned her. 'I shouldn't have kept you talking for so long this morning before you had your shower.'

The words, casual enough, caused Lucy to react so swiftly and so intimately that she was hotly ashamed of the responses of her body. This was an unfamiliar sensation for her. She was not used to experiencing these kind of feelings, to reacting so intensely to the most innocuous of remarks simply because they had been made by one particular man.

'Realising you'd been out running this morning made me realise how out of condition I've been getting recently. I used to run regularly myself.'

Lucy's heart leapt against her chest wall. He

wasn't going to suggest they they went running together, was he?

Quickly, frantically almost, she interrupted him.

'There's a very good gym opened at the golf club recently. It's very up-market...very well equipped.'

She stumbled over the last few words as she saw the way he had reacted to her comment about the gym's being up-market.

'If I was going to join a gym the bank-account balances of the other members wouldn't be what would interest me,' he told her grittily, almost angrily, she recognised.

'It might have been a theme of the last decade that wherever possible business was dragged into one's leisure activities, but that isn't the way I see things. As it happens, I don't actually like gym work, although I have been considering utilising some of the empty space we have at the unit to provide gym facilities for the staff.

'The work we're engaged in can be extremely mentally stressful, although physically it's exactly the opposite.'

'Perhaps, like you, your staff prefer not to take their exercise in a gym,' Lucy pointed out. She knew that she was being deliberately contrary; that what he was proposing showed that he was a committed and responsible employer, but she didn't *want* to acknowledge his virtues, she admitted mis-

erably. She didn't want to fall into the trap of slav-
ishly admiring everything he did.

'Maybe not, but at least that way they would
have the option.

'It's only a simple meal, I'm afraid,' he told her,
suddenly changing the subject. 'No starter, cold
salmon with salad and new potatoes, and then fruit
salad, plus cheese and biscuits.'

Lucy gave a small shrug and was startled by the
grim anger in his voice when he added sarcastically,
'But then you're not interested in food, are you?
Why do women have this ridiculous compulsion to
be thin, to destroy themselves and to deny their
femininity?'

His words irked Lucy, especially since in her
case they simply were not true.

'I have no idea,' she told him angrily. 'Perhaps
it has something to do with the fact that the male-
dominated advertising industry constantly bombards them with images of that kind of role model.'

'Just as it bombards us with muscle-bound ma-
cho types,' he pointed out to her. 'But I don't see
the male population collectively performing some
kind of lemming-like race towards self-destruction
in an attempt to emulate them.'

Lucy searched her brain for a crushing reply, but
could think of none other than a shaky, 'Over-
muscled men don't appeal to women.'

'And pin-thin women don't appeal to men, or at least not the majority of them.'

There was no doubt that he was including himself in that majority, she recognised. There had been just a hint of soft plumpness about Beth's face in the photograph, a hint perhaps that her body was similarly soft and rounded, the kind of body that to a man like Niall would immediately represent femininity, warmth, that would immediately arouse him to desire. There was undoubtedly a fecund softness about that kind of woman, a subtle, unspoken message of fertility that to a certain type of man was undoubtedly a very definite turn-on.

Well, *she* wasn't going to tell him that when she was under stress she just found it impossible to eat; that her slenderness was not something she prized and worked at, and that in fact she would have welcomed the addition of an extra half-stone of weight.

Let him disqualify her from the ranks of those women he found desirable. *She* didn't care. In fact, she was glad...relieved. She was *pleased*, in fact, that he had implied that he found her sexually unappealing.

Or so she told herself as she asked him distantly if there was anything she could do to help with the preparation of their lunch.

'No, it's all ready,' he told her cheerfully. 'If it had been warmer we could have eaten outside.

However, the dining-room does have a good view of the back garden, so I thought we'd eat in there.

'I'm afraid that as yet the house doesn't possess a downstairs cloakroom; in fact, the house is rather short of adequate bathroom facilities; there's a small shower-room off the room I'm using, and then one other bathroom. At the top of the stairs and then turn right. And the dining-room's this way,' he added, putting down the bowl of salad he had just removed from the fridge and coming towards her, opening the kitchen door for her and then directing her across the hallway and into a pretty panelled room via a door she hadn't noticed, tucked away to one side of the stairs.

The room wasn't large, but the panelling made her catch her breath in envy, and, as he had said, the room had a lovely view of the rear garden and the farmland beyond.

'It's still rather bare in here,' he apologised. 'No curtains as yet.'

No curtains maybe, but the furniture was good, Lucy recognised; a solid, sturdy table with eight matching chairs and an old dresser base standing against one of the panelled walls.

'The furniture belonged to my grandmother,' Niall told her, as though he had guessed what she was thinking.

'The chairs need re-covering, but in what I'm not

quite sure. Fortunately Beth isn't too keen. She prefers lighter, more delicate furniture.'

What did he mean, 'fortunately'? Lucy wondered as he excused himself to go and finish his preparations for their lunch.

Why should it please him that his lover didn't like his family furniture? She was still puzzling over this when he returned, pushing the trolley holding their lunch.

The meal he had prepared might only be simple, but the salad was crisply perfect, the tomatoes richly flavoured, the potatoes just as new potatoes ought to be, the salmon deliciously moist.

It was only when she had completely cleared her plate, eating with an enthusiasm she had not felt in a very long time, that Lucy realised he was watching her.

She avoided looking back at him, glad when he made no comment on her appetite.

It was just because she was eating with someone else...because they had been chatting so much that eating had been a pleasure rather than a lonely chore that underlined her aloneness, she told herself protectively.

And yet guiltily she acknowledged that so far Niall had not even raised the subject of the cottage. He had, in fact, she realised, been skilfully drawing her out to talk about her childhood, her teenage years, and then the years after that when she had been alone.

He had told her also something about his own childhood, about his feelings when he had lost his own mother, about his father's subsequent ill-health, and about how fortunate he recognised he had been to have had a grandmother strong enough and willing to hold the family together.

'I thought we'd have our coffee in the sitting-room,' he said when Lucy had finished her fruit salad and refused any cheese and biscuits.

'What about washing-up?' Lucy protested.

'It can go in the dishwasher,' he told her.

Five minutes later, settled in the comfortable warmth of the sitting-room settee, Lucy acknowledged that it might have been wiser to protest that they could conduct their business just as easily and certainly far less intimately over the dining-room table, but it was too late to make that comment now.

From where she was sitting she could see Beth's photograph.

Determinedly she focused on it, saying to Niall with a bright smile, 'You must miss Beth a great deal.'

He frowned slightly, as though he was either surprised or offended by her comment.

'In some ways,' he agreed.

'Do you know yet when she'll be coming back?' she pressed on.

'It depends on whether or not her secondment is extended for a further period,' he responded.

'Perhaps you could fly out to New York to see her,' she suggested. Two hectic spots of colour were burning on her cheeks. She could feel them and she knew quite well what the cause of them was.

'I could, but I doubt that I shall. New York...in fact, any city doesn't really appeal to me,' Niall told her briefly.

Lucy knew when she was beaten. It was plain that he didn't want to talk about Beth, but then why should he? *Their* relationship was a private thing, something which had nothing to do with her. She was merely an acquaintance, someone with whom he had been brought into contact because of his uncle.

'The cottage...' she began.

'The cottage,' Niall agreed. 'I've already told Eric that I've offered to buy it from you.'

'I expect he was pleased.'

It was all she could think of to say, to buy herself time while pride and necessity fought out their battle inside her.

'Not noticeably,' Niall told her drily.

Lucy looked at him in confusion.

'I don't think I properly understood the meaning of the description cantankerous until I met Eric. I suppose it's understandable, really. He's old and he's afraid, and, like all living things who experience fear, he's trying to defend himself.'

'Afraid.' Lucy's mouth compressed. 'I know he told you that I was threatening him,' she interrupted, 'but if he's implying that he's afraid of *me*...'

'That wasn't what I meant. I'm not a complete fool, Lucy,' Niall told her quietly. 'I *can* tell the difference between real and assumed emotions. No, when I said Eric was afraid, I meant that he was afraid of the unknown, of change, of losing the world that is familiar to him. *That's* why he doesn't want to leave the cottage. Oh, he won't admit it, not in so many words, but I'm sure that that is what's at the root of his refusal to move out, and of his insistence that he won't give up his tenancy. He knows that, the older he gets, the harder the social services are going to push him to move into some kind of sheltered accommodation, and while the cottage is in the condition it's in now it is a very real possibility that they will forcibly remove him for his own good.

'I suspect he's pinning his hopes on the fact that if the place was repaired they'd stop trying to get him to move out. Think about it. He's lived there virtually all his adult life.'

Lucy did. And to her shame she saw that Niall had seen an aspect of the situation which had totally escaped her. That he was displaying a compassion she had not possessed. A compassion that she, of all people, *ought* to have had.

'You really think that's the reason he's making all this fuss?' she asked Niall guiltily.

'As sure as I can be, given his remarkable stubborn, not to say at some times objectionable, attitude. Oh, yes, I do appreciate now that he *can* be objectionable,' he told her. 'A bit like a dog displaying antisocial aggression to mask its fear,' he added humorously.

There was an odd, uncomfortable lump in Lucy's throat. Why hadn't *she* seen that?

Was it because she had been too preoccupied with her own feelings, her own fear? Perhaps if she had taken the time and thought to try to understand Eric Barnes's position instead of reacting with such panic to his threats and demands...

But what difference would it have made? She *still* would not have been able to afford to have the repairs done.

But she would at least not be feeling the guilt that was now filling her.

'Half of me still says that he would be better off

living here, but another half of me acknowledges
that, while physically he might be better off, mentally he probably needs to feel that he is indepen-
dent, that he is in charge of his own life. If you
sold me the cottage I'd be able to allow him that
independence for a little while longer.'

How could she refuse after hearing that? Lucy
knew that, even if she had actually wanted to keep
the cottage, which she most certainly did not, she
could not have done so after listening to Niall's
grave speech.

'He'll still have to move out while the alterations
and repairs are being done,' she pointed out huskily.

'Very probably, but at least he will have the reassurance of knowing that he'll be moving back in
again.' Niall paused, refilled her coffee-cup before
she could protest, and then asked her, 'Am I to take
it from that that you *are* willing to sell to me?'

'I'd be a fool not to, wouldn't I?' Lucy replied
shakily, and then flushed at the way he looked at
her.

'If you're in agreement then I'll arrange to have
the place valued,' he told her.

'Is that really necessary?' Lucy asked him, adding with wry self-mockery, 'I have an uncomfortable feeling that any sane valuer will suggest that *I*
should pay *you* for taking it off my hands.'

'You mustn't overlook the fact that there could come a time in the future when the site might be a valuable building plot,' Niall warned her.

Lucy shook her head.

'I don't care about that. It's far too remote a possibility, and besides…'

'Besides what?' Niall pressed her.

Lucy shrugged uncomfortably.

'I know your uncle suspects that I wanted to keep the cottage for some ulterior motive, but I'm really not interested in any potential future value either it or the land might have. Inheriting it in the first place was such a shock. I had no idea that Emily still owned it.'

Something of what she had experienced was betrayed in her voice. She recognised it herself and knew that Niall was aware of it as well.

She pulled a brief face and said as briskly as she could, 'Heavens, I do sound full of self-pity, don't I?' She picked up her coffee-cup and drank the contents quickly.

'I really ought to go,' she told him, about to stand up. 'I know you must be busy, having just moved here.'

'Not really,' Niall told her, adding, 'Actually, there's something else I wanted to discuss with you. A favour I wanted to ask you, so to speak.'

He wanted a favour from *her*?

Lucy waited.

'It's this place,' he told her. 'Since Verity told me it lacked a woman's touch I've realised that she's quite right, and after seeing your home this morning...

'I was wondering if you'd be prepared to give *me* the benefit of your expertise and help me with this place.'

What expertise? was Lucy's first thought. Her second was a tiny thrill of apprehensive excitement, followed quickly by the realisation of exactly what was causing that feeling.

In order to quell it she said quickly, 'Oh, but surely Beth—?'

'Beth wouldn't be interested,' Niall told her. 'Besides, she's on the other side of the Atlantic. I know you can't have much time to spare and that it won't be an easy task. I've got to admit *I* wouldn't even know where to start, hence the lack of curtains in almost every room, and the fact that the dining-room chairs are still in need of re-covering.'

'You'd need a very traditional fabric,' Lucy murmured, her interest aroused despite the warning voice telling her she was getting into just the sort of situation she ought to avoid. 'Watts are very good for that kind of thing. Modern cottons are too light for this kind of setting; the colours always seem too harsh somehow.'

'So you will help me.'

Lucy gave him a quick unnerved look.

'I don't know... A home is so personal,' she began uncertainly. 'I'm not sure...'

She was standing up now, and so was Niall.

'I am,' he told her, and while the words were still reverberating through her skull he reached out and touched her, drawing his knuckles gently down the side of her face.

'You have such soft skin,' he told her quietly. 'It's so unbelievably sensitive. No, don't tense your muscles. There's nothing you need to fear.'

'I'm not afraid,' Lucy denied stoutly. 'Why should I be?'

'Why indeed?' Niall agreed.

He was, she realised, whispering the words against her lips, and the hand that had just touched her face was now resting warmly against her throat, somehow gently easing her head back so that he could brush his mouth slowly and tantalising against hers.

She had never realised that so light a touch could have such an intense reaction, she acknowledged.

She wanted to open her mouth, to let her lips cling to his, to touch him with her tongue, to see if he tasted the way her senses told her he would. She wanted to raise herself up on tiptoe and to press herself against him. She wanted to wrap her arms

around him, to feel the hardness of his chest against
her breasts. She wanted him to hold her and to
touch her, to stroke his hands down her back until
they found that vulnerable spot they had touched
this morning. She wanted to feel his touch against
her naked skin. She wanted him to want her, to tell
her and to show her that he found her desirable,
irresistible. She wanted to see and to touch his body
as well; to stroke her fingers over his chest, and
through the soft darkness of his body hair. She
wanted to feel his muscles contract with arousal
beneath that touch. She wanted to stroke his skin
with her tongue, to explore the alien flat hardness
of his nipples and to feel the corresponding surge
of sensation fill her own breasts as she did so.

She wanted *him*, she recognised helplessly as he
continued to kiss her slowly, savouringly, so that
her mouth opened for him completely of its own
volition, her body turning soft and fluid as he
cupped her face and held her while he kissed her
with such slow deepening sensuality that she was
fathoms out of her depth before she even realised
it.

She wanted him, wanted him so much that her
body openly vibrated and pulsed with that wanting
and she was helpless to do anything to stop it, and
he hadn't even touched her, hadn't done a single
thing to elicit the openly sensual trembling that con-

vulsed her. All he had done was to kiss her, to whisper against her mouth that the feel of her, the taste of her was driving him out of his mind.

His thumb-tip stroked the vulnerable hollow behind her ear. She trembled violently, drowning in the intense storm of feeling that erupted inside her, Beth totally forgotten, as his tongue thrust passionately into her mouth.

It was an act as dangerously erotic and almost as intimate as though he had actually possessed her, and her senses responded helplessly to it.

Without knowing how she had done so, she discovered that she was clutching him, her fingers digging into the flesh of his back. The flesh of his back...not his shirt, and yet she had no knowledge, no awareness, of having tugged the shirt out of his jeans, of having slid her hands beneath it, but she must have done so.

'Shall I tell you how much I wanted you this morning?' Niall was saying against her mouth. 'How much I wanted to share your shower with you, to take hold of you and touch you, to love you...?'

To *love* her... Her mind recognised the verb and retreated from it, but her senses were far too aroused for her to dwell on the small sharp pain that had momentarily jarred through her.

Niall was still kissing her, his mouth slowly exploring the line of her throat. He was also trying to push her away from him, she recognised.

She must have made a protest because he stopped moving, holding her still, while he kissed her slowly again and then whispered, 'It's all right...I just want to take this off.'

'This...' She gave him a dazed look and realised that he was removing his shirt.

'And this,' he told her, speaking quietly, as quietly as someone might to a half-wild nervous creature. As though his tone had soothed her, Lucy stood still while he removed her jacket.

'Do you know what I was thinking while I waited for you this morning?' she heard him saying softly to her.

'I was thinking how much I wanted to feel the silky warmth of your breasts against my body. I was trying not to imagine how it would feel to take your nipple into my mouth and to suck on it until you cried out with pleasure.'

He wasn't just removing her jacket, Lucy realised with dazed awareness. He was removing her top as well, and her skirt, and she wasn't doing a single thing to stop him. She didn't *want* to stop him, because all she could think about was the mental images conjured up by his huskily rough words. Already her body was responding shamelessly to him, and she knew that when he removed her bra,

as she knew he was going to do, her nipples would
be as hard and as sensitively swollen as though he
had in fact already drawn them into his mouth and
suckled on their eager peaks.

He was holding her closely now, stroking her
back, tenderly exploring the slope of her shoulder
with lips that seemed to know exactly where to lin-
ger, where to exert that little bit more pressure, until
she shuddered in frantic response.

'I want to take you upstairs. To make love to you
slowly and lingeringly in the privacy and the comfort of my bed, but if I stay here with you like this
for much longer...'

Lucy felt the shudder galvanise his body and
knew it was caused by his desire for her. Her heart
leapt with joy, her body pulsingly eager to respond
to the messages of his.

Picking up his shirt, Niall gently put it on her,
his hands resting lightly against her breasts very
briefly as he leaned forward and kissed her, a slow,
almost tender kiss that for some reason made her
want to cry, her throat tight with choking emotion.

The fabric of his shirt felt soft against her skin.
Somehow because he had worn it it was almost as
though in some erotic way *he* was actually touching
her. She was conscious of his scent clinging to the
fabric. She trembled as he fastened the button between her breasts, her nipples peaking urgently, her

breath catching in her throat as she felt the aching swell of desire to have his hands touching her.

'Come on,' he said slowly against her mouth. 'Let's go upstairs.'

With his arm around her, holding her against his side, he guided her into the hall and up the stairs. Halfway up them he stopped and turned to look at her, an odd sombre look that made her heart beat heavily with painful anxiety.

His arm was still around her. He lifted his free hand and touched her face, almost as an adult might touch a child, she recognised.

'Lucy, I want you to know—' he began, and then stopped as she silenced whatever it was he was about to say by pushing herself against him and lifting her mouth to his, kissing him with an almost desperate ferocity.

She felt the shock tense his body, and then both his arms tightened around her and he was kissing her back.

She had no idea what he had intended to say to her. She only knew that she didn't want to hear it; that she didn't want to hear anything that might destroy the shining fragility of what she was feeling.

He carried her the rest of the way up the stairs and into a large low-ceilinged bedroom where the eaves sloped down to a pair of small dormer windows.

The floorboards were bare and polished, dark with age and uneven, and the room still retained an opening where once there must have been a fireplace.

Opposite it was the bed, high and old-fashioned with a heavy wrought-iron bedstead, its white linen covers worn with age.

When Niall placed her carefully on the bed the linen felt soft against her skin.

As he kissed her Niall told her, 'I won't be a moment.' He was gone before she could query *where* he was going.

She stared round the room, her eyes huge and round as though she was half unable to believe what was happening.

On the oak chest between the two dormer windows was a photograph in a silver frame. Her heart started to thump frantically as she stared at it.

'My grandparents,' Niall told her, coming back into the room and observing her.

Lucy didn't want to acknowledge why she felt so relieved at the composition of the photograph, at the fact that it was of two people and not one.

Niall, she realised as she looked at him, was carrying her clothes, and as he carefully placed them on the chair beside the chest she was overwhelmed by the strongest surge of emotion she had ever experienced.

It wasn't just desire she felt for him, she acknowledged as her eyes suddenly burned with tears. It was love as well. He was so caring, so compassionate, so aware, that how could she not have loved him? She blinked, the emotion that filled her blotting out everything else.

She was still wearing his shirt, and now as he came over to the bed he teased her gently.

'Mm...I'm glad you kept this on.'

Foolishly perhaps, or perhaps because suddenly she felt oddly nervous, almost shy, she didn't immediately sense what he meant, and asked him uncertainly, 'Why?'

He laughed then, his eyes warm with pleasure as he looked at her.

'So that I can undo it, of course,' he told her as he kissed the side of her throat and then the hollow at its base when her pulse raced so frantically, and then lower into the open V of his shirt, while his hands smoothed up over her body beneath the shirt, their touch warm against the curve of her hips, shaping the narrowness of her waist.

Her breath caught in her throat as she waited for the moment when his hands and his lips would reach the same point, knowing that her breasts were already shamelessly flaunting their need.

The sensation of his lips slowly caressing the hollow between her breasts while his hands cupped their swollen softness made her cry out, her body arching fiercely against him, her hands going out to hold his head.

If he had not done it for her she knew that she would have wrenched off the shirt herself, guiding his mouth to her aching flesh, but he seemed to know instinctively how she felt, how she ached, and the touch of his lips, at first gentle and explorative, very quickly became far less controlled, far more demanding as he felt her response to him.

The sharp spasms of sensation that pierced through her made Lucy cry out and reach up to him, holding him against her body, a tumble of incoherent words smothered against his skin as she pressed her face against him, too caught up in what she was experiencing to have room to feel anything other than a brief sense of shock that she could actually feel like this, abandon herself like this.

The ache deep within her body demanded the pressure of Niall's weight against her, but, even as she acknowledged that need herself, Niall responded to it, his hand stroking down over her body, cupping her, holding her, while he slowly relinquished her nipple, caressing it soothingly with his tongue before easing her back against the bed and then kneeling over her, watching her.

'I want you so much,' he told her sombrely. 'Tell me you want me as well, Lucy.'

'I want you.'

She said it softly, immediately, without any desire to conceal or deny her need of him, so totally at ease with him, somehow made so confident of her femininity and her desirability to him, that she felt no need to hold back or to pretend.

He cupped her face, his hands sliding into her hair as he unfastened her plait.

She felt him shudder and saw the dark flush of colour stain his skin, and she marvelled that she could have this effect on him.

She watched silently as he removed the rest of their clothes and then caught her breath, her face flushing a little at her own naïve response to his nakedness until she saw in his eyes how much her reaction to him had pleased him.

'Don't,' he told her as she instinctively tried to turn away. 'I like seeing that you want me. I like knowing that my body arouses you as powerfully as yours does me.

'Tell me what you want, Lucy,' he murmured to her as he leaned over her. 'Tell me how you want me to touch you...to make love to you.'

Lucy closed her eyes, shaken by the surge of knowledge that she didn't just want him to touch her, she wanted to touch him as well.

It was a need she simply could not put into words; instead she reached out and touched his skin, her fingertips hesitant and uncertain as they traced the corded muscle on the inside of his arm. Totally bemused by the sensation of his skin, she raised herself up and placed her mouth against it.

She hadn't realised that a man could tremble so violently, she thought in awe as he groaned her name, hadn't realised how the most tentative touch could weaken his masculine control.

Nor had she realised how good it would be to taste his skin, to draw her open mouth against the muscled hardness of his chest, to flick her tongue hesitantly at first and then more surely against the tight hardness of his nipple while he cried out and gripped hold of her, his body suddenly slick with sweat, his muscles corded with response.

When he touched her, intimately seeking the moist invitation of her body, she arched up against him, pressing herself fiercely against his hand, telling him feverishly and openly how much she wanted him, how much her body craved the satin strength of his.

It had been a long time since she had last made love, and then it had never been like this; then she had never come anywhere near experiencing this intensity of arousal, and yet as Niall moved against and then within her she was so exquisitely conscious of him that she cried out in shock, her eyes wide open as she met the burning intensity of his.

It wasn't pain that made her cry out, her dizzied brain acknowledged, it was a sensation, a pleasure so unknown and yet immediately so recognised and welcomed by her body that it instantly adapted itself to Niall's special rhythm, responding to it and to him as though it had been born to do so.

Afterwards as Niall held her, stroking her, soothing her, whispering murmured words against her skin, she clung desperately to him, her heart aching with the weight of all that she didn't want to acknowledge, while her body ached with the pleasure he had shown it.

Later Niall made love to her again, touching her, kissing her with an intimacy she had never dreamed she would ever want to share with anyone, never mind feel a fierce need to actually experience.

The taste of her own body on his mouth when he kissed her was powerfully erotic, making her ache to share the same intimacy with him, to experience the texture and the taste of his most essential maleness.

When Lucy finally fell asleep in Niall's arms her face was still damp from the tears of happiness she had cried as he had loved her.

LUCY WOKE UP abruptly, her heart pounding frantically. She had been having a bad dream; a dream in which she had been confronted by a white-faced, distraught Beth, accusing her of trying to steal her lover.

Beth! Lucy shuddered, sick with shame and shock, crawling to the edge of the bed, unable to bear the knowledge of what she had done, unable even to look at Niall, still sleeping and oblivious to her anguish.

She had to get away from him, from this room with its sickening memories of what she had done, of how she had pleaded and cried out, of how she had silently whispered her love, while all the time refusing to acknowledge that she had no right to express that love.

Niall was committed to another woman. To Beth. She had known that fact and she had wilfully, selfishly ignored it.

Sickness washed over her as she struggled into her clothes. She was trembling so much that she could hardly move. She prayed that Niall wouldn't wake up. He was a man, she tormented herself, and men were notorious for not always being able to control their sexual desires, but she was a *woman*; and a woman moreover who had always prided herself not only on her self-control, but also for her refusal to allow herself to become involved in any way with a man who was involved with someone else. She *despised* the kind of woman who allowed herself to become a party to a man's deception of his partner. She had *always* believed that she was far too strong *ever* to become involved in that kind of situation; that she had too much pride, too much self-respect to allow a man to use her in that way.

And it had certainly never once occurred to her that *she* might actually fall in love with such a man. As far as she was concerned, trust and respect were two essential pillars for any intimate, loving relationship, and how could they exist between two people of whom one was cheating on someone else while the other was aware of it?

Once dressed, she crept quietly out of the bedroom and downstairs, using the telephone to ring for a taxi, and telling the driver she would meet him at the end of the lane.

On her way out of the sitting-room she caught the glint of the silver frame holding Beth's photograph.

Guilt, remorse, self-loathing; she felt them all, and with them a panicky sense of disbelief that it had actually happened...that *she* had actually allowed...no, not allowed, her mind corrected her mercilessly, encouraged, invited, incited Niall to make love to her. It was quite obvious to her now that he had planned to do so from the moment he had invited her to lunch.

Why... why had she allowed such a thing to happen?

She let herself out of the house, welcoming the cold sting of the night air against her face, achingly aware that the burden of her guilt was something she would never lose. She had done something she had always sworn she would never do, and no amount of guilt, of self-recrimination could ever change that.

As she stumbled down the lane towards the main road and her waiting taxi she told herself that she must never, *ever* see Niall again.

It didn't matter that logic told her that *he* was equally to blame; that *he* had known just as much as she that he was not free to make love to her: the major burden of the blame lay with her. Beth was a member of her own sex. Another woman. A woman who loved and trusted Niall. Lucy shuddered nauseously.

Oh, God, what had she *done*? She could feel the acid sting of her own tears and brushed them quickly away. She might well cry, but a river of tears couldn't wash away her guilt. And it was no excuse that she loved Niall. None at all.

She writhed in mental agony as she remembered the number of times she had both inwardly and outwardly expressed the view that love was never an excuse for breaking moral laws; that there must always come a point in any relationship where one knew that to go any further would be breaking those laws, where one had the opportunity to draw back.

The taxi driver took one look at her set, tear-stained face and made no attempt to engage her in conversation.

Lucy thanked him when she paid his fare and then walked stiffly, as though suddenly she had aged and grown tired with life, towards her apartment.

As she stripped off and scrubbed her skin beneath the sting of the shower, she prayed that Beth would never know what had happened; that she would be spared that final burden.

But then there was no reason why she should know, she assured herself. After all, Niall was hardly likely to tell her. She tensed, wondering sickly how often he had done this before. The nausea rose up inside her, making her want to scour her body, to punish it for what it had done.

What she had in her naïveté interpreted as tenderness had obviously merely been experience; where she had seen gentleness, compassion and concern, *he* had merely been exhibiting his knowledge of female arousal, female emotions. Where *she* had thought there was passionate desire for her there had in actual fact been only a male desire for sex.

She had deluded herself shamelessly and she deserved every second of misery and despair she was now going to have to endure. And the worst punishment of all was the knowledge that she loved him.

Yes, that was definitely the worst punishment of all.

CHAPTER EIGHT

IT WAS the ring of the telephone beside her bed that woke Lucy out of a heavy, nightmare-infested sleep.

She reached automatically for the receiver and then stopped, staring at the instrument while the blood congealed heavily in her veins and her heart thudded slowly and sickly.

It might not, of course, be Niall who was ringing her, but she could not afford to take that chance.

She got out of bed, wrenching the telephone power point from its socket. The ringing ceased immediately, although she could still hear the trill of the downstairs phone.

It was just gone half-past six. She tried to imagine Niall waking up to find her missing, wondering where she was, searching the house perhaps and then finally realising that she wasn't there; picking up the phone.

To do what? To implore her to go back, or to reassure himself that she understood that for him last night had simply been a brief journey down a sexual side-road that led nowhere?

Either way, she didn't want to speak with him. Or dared not allow herself to speak with him, a bitter voice challenged her. She, who had been so proud, so sure that she would never never be caught in the trap of loving a man who wasn't free to love her in return.

The last thing she felt like doing was going to work. She knew she could ring Don and claim to be unwell and that he would not even question or doubt her, but if she stayed at home...if Niall had been telephoning her...

She shuddered, the fear and rage that filled her galvanising her into action.

Half an hour later, showered and dressed, she dried her hair and put on her make-up.

Downstairs she made herself some breakfast— coffee and wholemeal toast. Her gorge rose with every mouthful of food, but she forced herself to keep on eating.

As she checked her appearance before she left for work she wondered if the tension *she* could see clearly in her face would be equally obvious to others. If so she would just have to hope that they would put it down to her anxiety over the cottage.

The cottage. She froze. What was she going to do about that now? The last thing she wanted was any kind of contact with Niall, but as her thoughts twisted frantically, seeking an alternative way out, she knew that, as far as the cottage was concerned, any decisions were not now hers to make.

She had agreed to sell it to Niall. Whether he still wished to buy it or whether, like her, any future contact between them was something he wanted to completely avoid, she could do nothing other than abide by his choice.

She was simply not in a position to withdraw her acceptance of his offer to buy the place, she recognised sickly.

She left for work much earlier than usual, anxious for something, anything, that would keep her thoughts occupied.

She had her own key for the offices and she let herself in. She had been there less than fifteen minutes when the phone started to ring. She picked up the receiver automatically and then tensed as she heard Niall demanding urgently, 'Lucy, thank goodness... What's wrong? *Why* did you leave without waking me? I must see you.'

She had thought she was prepared for the pain she would suffer, but now, listening to him, her mind tormenting her with memories of how he had touched her, the things he had said to her, the things she had said to him, she knew that there was nothing that could possibly armour her against what she was feeling, and added to her guilt was a slow, aching tide of despair.

'Lucy.'

Her silence must have got through to him because she heard the charged tension in his voice as he said her name.

The temptation simply to put down the receiver almost overwhelmed her, but she withstood it, knowing that it would be an act of cowardice.

'I don't want to see you, Niall,' she told him. 'There isn't any point.'

She heard the explosive sound he made so clearly that she might almost have been in the room beside him. Was he dressed, or was he standing as he had done last night, his skin sleek and supple, his body so overpoweringly male that even now, and despite all her self-loathing and guilt, she could actually feel the fierce tingle of awareness that marked her response to him?

'No point? What?' She could hear something that was almost confusion in his voice. 'Lucy, please—'

'No, I don't want to see you or speak to you ever again,' she told him fiercely, suddenly terrified by the way she could feel her resolve weakening.

Already she was aching for him, emotionally as well as physically. The telephone receiver felt slippery in her damp hand. She wanted to cry out to him; to beg him to reassure her, to tell her that there was no other woman in his life, like a child crying in the darkness to be comforted.

But for her there could be no comfort, only the agony of facing up to the truth.

Silently she replaced the receiver.

It was done. Over. She had left no room for any going back, but at lunchtime, when her head was pounding with the kind of headache that no amount of pills could take away, and Don had already commented with some concern on her wan appearance, she looked up from her work to see Niall standing in the open doorway of her office, a grimly determined expression on his face.

'I want to talk to you,' he told her unequivocally.

'I was just going out for my lunch,' she told him unsteadily.

'Fine,' he accepted, tight-lipped. 'I'll come with you, although I doubt that you'll want anyone else to overhear what I have to say to you.'

He meant it, Lucy realised. There was no sign now of yesterday's gentleness, yesterday's compassion; in its place was an implacable determination and banked-down anger that made her heart beat in triple time.

She didn't speak. She didn't need to. Her expression gave her away. She glanced helplessly from Niall's set face to the open door. He smiled mirthlessly at her, and closed it with a sharp thud.

'Very wise,' he approved.

And then he walked over to her desk.

If she had thought that keeping the width of it between them offered her some measure of safety she realised that she had been wrong. As he leaned across it, his palms flat on its top either side of her blotter, she recognised how easily he could reach just that little bit further and pluck her completely out of her chair.

'I want to know what the hell is going on,' he told her through gritted teeth. 'Last night…'

Last night. Every muscle in Lucy's body tensed. She looked at him, her eyes dull with self-loathing.

'Last night should never have happened,' she told him shakily.

'Why not?' he challenged. 'Aren't you human just like the rest of us? Aren't *any* emotions allowed into that sterile, empty heart of yours? Aren't you allowed to feel or to want? Well, it's too late for pretence now, Lucy. Last night you wanted me and—'

'No!'

She screamed the denial frantically at him, but he ignored it, continuing brutally, 'No? Did I imagine it, then, when you told me how much you wanted me, how much you wanted my hands on your body, my mouth? Did I imagine it when you begged me to let you touch me, when your body quivered with desire at the sight of mine? Face it, Lucy, you are a human being, no matter how much you want to deny it; and part of being a human being involves feeling human emotions. And you're lying if you deny now that, last night in my arms, you felt those emotions.

'I know how much you suffered when you lost your parents, but you can't go through the rest of your life shunning any kind of emotional contact because of that. You're such a coward, Lucy, do you know that? A coward and a fraud. And don't worry,' he added icily, 'I haven't come here to plead with you or to beg. The last thing I want is a woman coming to me reluctantly, denying her feelings.'

He stood up and walked over to the door, opening it and striding through it, and then closing it behind him.

All the time Lucy sat where she was, completely unable to move.

His attack on her had been so unexpected that she had been completely unprepared for it.

She had expected him to question why she had left, but she had also expected him to make it plain to her at the same time what they both knew, namely that he was involved with someone else.

Now that he had gone his words echoed through her mind, hurtful, cruel words, which nevertheless held a gritty kernel of truth. She had been like that—afraid of emotion, afraid to get involved, but yesterday, in his arms, she had lost that fear, had simply left it behind her, shedding it as easily and as freely as she had shed her clothes, and with as little regret, and it hurt her unbearably now that he had not recognised that, that he had not seen... recognised just what she was giving him.

Now, as she forced back the tears burning the backs of her eyes, she was thankful that Don was out seeing a client and that no one had overheard them.

She *had* done the right thing, she assured herself. Loving him hurt and would go on hurting, but that was *her* problem.

To have continued seeing him... No...she could never allow herself to be guilty of that kind of deceit.

That night, unable to sleep, she thumped her pillow and told herself that he was not worth a single one of her tears. If he had, even if only fleetingly, acknowledged Beth's role in his life, if he had expressed remorse or guilt...but he had simply never mentioned her, behaved as though she did not even exist. And then to accuse *her*, to behave as though...as though she were rejecting his love...a love they both knew he neither felt nor was free to give...

She hated him, she told herself fiercely as the tears soaked her pillow. She hated him...hated him.

Three days later she received a letter from Niall's solicitor, making her a formal offer for the cottage which, in view of its condition, was ridiculously high.

What was he doing? Trying to buy her off? Conscience money? Even while her brain, her intelligence told her that it wasn't so, her emotions refused to listen. She wanted to be able to fan her anger against him, to feed her hatred. She needed that defence, that protection, she recognised bleakly.

On Saturday morning when she woke up the moment she lifted her head off the pillow she felt dizzyingly sick.

She hadn't been eating properly all week. Food was the last thing she had wanted, even while common sense had warned her that she must eat.

By the time she reached the bathroom the nausea had subsided, but it recurred later when she got up, her body cold and clammy, as she shook and trembled with sickness.

Her hand on her stomach, she told herself that she must have picked up some kind of virus, but another very different fear haunted the back of her mind, a fear she dared not allow herself to explore.

Just as three days later she refused to allow herself to acknowledge the terror that was now a leaden, petrifying lump of dread paralysing every aspect of her life when her period, normally so regular, so reliable, failed to materialise with its routine smoothness.

She couldn't possibly be pregnant, she told herself, and then, as the panic imploded inside her, she found herself praying feverishly, Please, God, don't let me be pregnant.

Taking any kind of steps to prevent conception had been the last thing on her mind when Niall had made love to her. Feverishly she even acknowledged that, had the thought occurred to her, such had been her state of arousal and desire, her love, that she would all too probably have welcomed the possibility.

A child of her own. Hot tears stung her eyes. There was nothing she would like more. Already she could see the small downy head nestling against her breast, the round baby-blue eyes. Already she could feel the baby skin, smell the baby scent. She could even feel the small betraying contraction of her womb as it responded to her thoughts.

A child. *Niall's* child, unplanned, perhaps, but never, ever unwanted, at least not by her.

But how *could* she have Niall's child? How *could* she bring it up, living in such proximity to Niall and to Beth? Beth, who had done nothing to deserve the suffering she would have, that would torment her, if she ever found out that Niall had fathered another woman's child.

And what of her child, growing up, unable to know the identity of its father, her guilt eating into her as she was forced to refuse its pleas to know something about the other half of itself?

And she and Niall, bound together by their mutual guilt. No, none of it could be allowed to happen. She could see so clearly the pain, the misery they would all face down the years because of that single selfish act she and Niall had shared.

But what was the alternative? To destroy her child? To deny it life?

Helplessly she knew that was something she could never do. She would have to go away, to make a life for herself somewhere else, and quickly, before anyone realised what was happening. Their town was such a small place. She could not even go into a chemist's shop and buy a pregnancy-testing kit without causing speculation and gossip.

She would have to go into Chester...somewhere anonymous. Her mind raced frantically on while her hand still rested protectively against her stomach.

With this new problem to face, the cottage and Niall's letter were pushed completely out of her mind.

Niall had made no further attempts to contact her and she knew that he had accepted her denial of him.

Probably with relief, she told herself cynically, although it had not been relief or anything remotely like it which had brought him so furiously into her office to accuse her of cowardice.

Would he think her a coward now for not destroying his child?

What did it matter what he thought? she challenged herself, acknowledging that she spent far too much time thinking about him, dwelling on what she had shared with him, and, even worse, wanting him.

The knowledge that she loved him was the most painful burden she had ever had to bear. How *could* she love someone like that…a man who cheated on a woman he was supposed to love…a man who casually had sex with a woman for whom he felt nothing more than a brief passing desire?

She ought to loathe and despise him. Instead of which she loved him, and loathed and despised herself.

She was thinking about him as she drove home from work that night, and about her child…her child…her thoughts so intimate, so emotionally disturbing that the sight of him leaning, arms folded, against his Discovery, waiting for her, sent a charge of such jolting sensation through her that it was almost like an electric shock.

There was no way she could avoid him. A coward, he had called her; well, she wasn't going to prove it to him, she decided as she parked her car and got out, praying that her shaking legs would support her.

He didn't waste any time. As soon as she was within earshot he demanded tersely, 'What exactly are you playing at, Lucy? Why haven't you responded to my solicitor's letter?'

His letter. She had forgotten all about it, and the flush of guilt that stained her face proclaimed that fact too obviously for her to deny it.

Immediately Niall frowned and, unfolding his arms, took a step towards her.

'What's wrong?' he demanded tersely. 'You don't look well.'

It was more than she could endure. Immediately her eyes flashed brilliant with anger and suppressed tears.

'Oh, really? I hadn't noticed,' she told him sarcastically, and then, unable to stop herself, added in a tormented husky voice, 'How do you expect me to feel? How am I supposed to feel?' To her horror, she could hear her voice thickening with tears. Another moment and she would be breaking down completely.

'You called me a coward, Niall,' she told him, fighting to remind herself of exactly what he was. 'Well, at least that's all I am.'

'Meaning?' he demanded, watching her.

He was standing far too close to her, Lucy recognised numbly, but she wasn't going to give him the satisfaction of moving, of letting him know how perilous her hold over her self-control really was, and how much she ached, longed simply to fling herself in his arms and to beg him to hold her.

'Meaning that *I* might be a coward, but I won't be guilty of ruining someone else's life, or destroying their trust, of—'

'Who the hell are you talking about?' Niall interrupted her impatiently.

Lucy gave him a bitter, scornful look.

'Beth, of course,' she told him quietly.

'Beth?'

Niall stared at her and then repeated, astounded, 'Beth? Just what in God's name does she have to do with us?'

She had known all along, of course…had known what lay behind the outward caring, the outward display of emotions and feelings that had drawn her so self-destructively to him. Had known all along that they must be…that they *had* to be a sham, but to hear him confirm it so brutally and so uncaringly shocked her into numb silence.

If, in any tiny corner of her mind, she had clung to the hope not that he would deny Beth or her place in his heart, but that he would tell her that he genuinely felt he had made a mistake, that he had genuinely loved Beth, but that that love had died even before he had met her then now she knew what folly that had been.

What has Beth to do with us? he had said, and she knew sickly that for him there was no guilt, no pain, no remorse, because to him she and Beth occupied two very different places in his life.

From somewhere she managed to find the strength to twist her mouth into what she hoped looked like a smile. And, praying that her voice wouldn't crack and betray her completely, she told him huskily, 'Nothing...since there is no us.'

She made to step past him, tensing as he put out a hand to detain her.

'Don't touch me, Niall,' she warned him, and something in her face must have reached him, have touched some part of him, because he immediately withdrew, his mouth curving downwards into a grimly hard line of anger.

'Don't touch me,' he repeated harshly. 'That wasn't what you said the night you shared my bed.'

She supposed that she deserved it, and she certainly wasn't going to deny it, could not deny it.

Instead she told him in a small, dead voice, 'I'm

sorry I didn't respond to your solicitor's letter.
Naturally I'm willing to go ahead with the sale.'
And, keeping as far away from him as she possibly
could, she turned her back on him and walked
away, holding her breath in case he followed her.

He didn't, of course, but then why should he?
Alone in her flat, she sat down in a chair and closed
her eyes. Had he really expected that she would
continue to see him…that she would continue to
sleep with him, knowing about Beth?

And if he did, was it entirely his fault? she tormented herself grimly.

If she had stuck to her principles from the first,
if she had simply and firmly made it plain to him
that, no matter how much he might be able to
arouse her, she was not…could not become his
lover then none of this would have happened.

Oh, she might still have loved him, useless to try
to deny that, but the rest, her guilt, her despair…her
pregnancy…they would not have been there.

Her pregnancy. Hot tears stung her eyes. It was
all wrong to bring a child into the world in this
way, and yet she couldn't help loving it, just as she
hadn't been able to help loving its father.

Would her child come to hate her, to blame her?
The tears trickled down her face. She knew she was
being foolish and emotional; that she was torturing
herself now as a way of punishing herself for the

weakness; the need she had felt when she had seen Niall.

What has Beth to do with us? he had demanded. She shuddered sickly, knowing that if hearing that comment had not killed her love and made her face up to the truth then nothing would.

CHAPTER NINE

'YOU want me to go to France?' Lucy questioned.

'Mm,' Don told her. 'Edward Jenkins phoned me at home last night in something of a panic. There seems to be some problem with the finance for the manor-house they're buying. Knowing Edward, I suspect that part of the cause lies with him. He does tend to have rather an unfortunate manner.'

'Mm…the kind of Englishman who believes if he shouts loudly enough in a foreign country he must be able to make himself understood,' Lucy agreed.

'I'd go myself, but there isn't much point. My French is nowhere near as good as yours, and you know the situation, the people down there.'

It was true and Lucy couldn't deny it, and besides…if she went to France she wouldn't run the risk of seeing Niall. She wouldn't be constantly dreading the ring of her phone, or arriving home to find him waiting for her—or arriving home not to find him waiting for her, she acknowledged miserably.

'It's all going to be a bit of a rush, I'm afraid,' Don told her. 'You'd have to leave this afternoon, hire a car from the airport and make contact with Edward as quickly as you could. According to him, they're virtually in danger of being evicted unless the situation's resolved pretty quickly. You know they're only renting the place until all the legal and financial ramifications can be sorted out, and now it seems there's another buyer in the offing.'

Lucy gave him a brief smile.

'I don't mind,' she told him truthfully, and then added much less truthfully, 'After all, there's nothing to keep me here.'

She went home first, packed a small suitcase, and then headed for the airport.

Driving in France was an experience that demanded strong nerves and an even stronger stomach, and right now Lucy acknowledged that she possessed neither, but somehow she made it safely to her destination.

She was booked into a local hotel, and before leaving home she had arranged to meet Edward and his wife for dinner so that she could discuss with them the problems they were experiencing.

Edward was inclined to be short-tempered and less than tactful. Emma, his wife, was much quieter, rather downtrodden, in fact. Lucy remembered that

when she had first met them she had felt rather
sorry for them.

Edward plainly considered himself to be something of a ladies' man and had tried relentlessly to
flirt with her. He wasn't one of her favourite people
by any means, but right now she was feeling almost
grateful towards him. At least here in France she
was safe, or, rather, safer. Not so much from Niall,
but from her own foolish emotions.

Perhaps she should uproot herself and make her
home here permanently, she reflected grimly as she
stripped off her clothes and walked into the shower.

It was only an idle thought; one which had had
no basis in reality, and yet it took root and flour-
ished.

Here there would be no chance of her child ever
discovering the truth, nor of Beth realising who had
fathered it. Here she would be free to create for her
child a father whose life had ended tragically before
its birth if she chose. Here she would be safe, free
from the tormenting memories and desires that
filled her at home.

All the time she was working, listening to
Edward's complaints, tactfully seeking meetings
with the French authorities and with the owner of
the property, soothing their ruffled feelings, speaking to them in her fluent elegant French, she was
thinking about the future. And not just her future,

but her child's, the future they would share together...just the two of them.

And then the day she was due to fly back home she woke up in the morning to discover that there was not after all to be a child.

She cried then, bitter, painful tears that echoed the grief she had felt when she had lost her parents.

Was she doomed to suffer like this throughout her life, to always lose where she loved?

First her parents, and now this. And it didn't matter that the child had never existed other than in her imagination, and that she had never been pregnant at all but merely suffering her body's reaction to her emotional and mental stress.

Of Niall she dared not let herself think at all. She had no right to think of him, she told herself fiercely. Not when there was Beth, and there always would be Beth.

Even if improbably he was to come to her now and tell her that it was over, that he was free to love her, *she* would never be free of her own burden of guilt, of knowing that her happiness was the cause of another woman's pain.

BACK AT HOME, she worked mechanically through the rest of the week, accepting Don's praise for what she had achieved with a brief smile but no real awareness.

She was functioning like an automaton, grimly holding on to the routine of her life as though without it she feared that it...that *she* would fall apart.

Verity rang her to remind her that she had promised to join the committee to organise the annual summer fête.

'The first meeting's next week,' she told her. 'In the church hall.'

Blankly Lucy promised to be there and dutifully made a note in her diary.

Tom rang her to announce that he and Josy were getting back together.

'It's the kids, really,' he confided to Lucy. 'They kept on begging me to come home. Neither of us is sure how it's going to work out, but at least we're both willing to give it a try.'

The weekend came and went; the nights were much lighter now and a restlessness possessed her. She found it difficult to settle to anything; even her home no longer had the power to soothe and comfort her.

She ached physically for Niall, but that was something she could control, just; what was far worse was her emotional longing for him.

It made no difference how often she reminded herself of what he was. Her heart refused to listen, and yet she knew that even if he had loved her it would have made no difference; that, even if she had given in to her love for him, sooner or later her guilt would have destroyed their relationship.

It wasn't pride that gave her that knowledge; she had no pride left now. She had come to realise far too bitterly just how meagre her moral strengths were when faced with the compelling force of her love. No, it wasn't pride that burned into her an awareness that there was no possibility of any kind of happy ending, it was just her own knowledge of herself.

On Monday evening the restlessness which had possessed her all weekend drove her out of her apartment and into her car.

She drove for miles, determinedly avoiding going anywhere near where Niall lived, and then somehow found that she was driving past the cottage.

Eric Barnes would, of course, have to be standing in his garden. It was obvious that he had recognised her car because he signalled to her to stop, and automatically she did so, tensing as he came towards her.

What sins was he about to accuse her of now? she wondered as he approached her.

'Nice evening,' he commented, startling her. Was that actually a smile she could see?

'Er—yes,' she agreed. 'Very pleasant.'

She had the car windows down, as it was a warm evening, and now he leaned against the passenger-door, for all the world as though they were old friends, Lucy recognised in bewilderment.

'Heard that you'd agreed to sell this place to that nephew of mine.'

Was that really embarrassment she could hear behind the casual, or rather almost hesitant comment?

She heard him clearing his throat. He looked away from her and added, 'Seems I might have been wrong about you.'

Lucy stared at him, almost unable to believe her ears.

'Thought you wanted me out of here,' he continued brusquely. 'Thought you were planning to get those social services people in on me, moving me out... They mean well enough, I suppose,' he admitted grudgingly. 'But I like living here. Always have lived here, see...and seems to me that I'm like to die here. But not for a good while yet. At least not if that nephew of mine gets the place fixed up like he's promised to.'

'I'm sure he will,' Lucy responded automatically.

Eric Barnes cleared his throat again, and this time he looked directly at her as he told her almost fiercely, 'You could come round and see it if you like, when it's all done. Says he's going to arrange for someone to come in and do a bit of cleaning for me. Not that I can't manage on my own,' he added, and told her, 'Says he's going to get someone in to see to the garden as well. He's a good lad.'

'Yes,' Lucy agreed, quickly blinking away her tears. Why, oh, why did there have to be this dichotomy in Niall's nature, and why now, when she could least bear it, must she be brought face to face with that other side of him, that caring, concerned, gentle side of him?

That night she dreamed about him, about the way he had touched her, about his tenderness and his care, about her own need for him and about all the things he had made her feel, and in her sleep she cried out for him, the sound of her own voice waking her to reality and the salt taste of the tears running down her face.

CHAPTER TEN

'OH, BY the way, I forgot to tell you, Niall Cameron rang asking for you while you were away.'

Lucy's heart somersaulted uncomfortably inside her chest. She was glad that Don was standing beside her and that he couldn't see her face.

'I expect it was something about the cottage. I'm selling it to him,' she told him huskily.

Of course, she had to explain then to Don about Niall's offer to buy the cottage from her, and when she had finished, he approved, 'The ideal solution from everyone's point of view. You must be feeling immensely relieved.'

Lucy gave him a brief meaningless smile. If she told Don exactly how she did feel he would be both shocked and embarrassed.

Bleakly she acknowledged that, even if there had been someone close enough to her emotionally for her to share her pain with, she would not have been able to do so. How could she when it would mean revealing how she had behaved?

It made no difference, telling herself that it was

because she loved him. That was no real excuse, at least not in her eyes.

She had to get on with her life, she told herself fiercely. She had to forget what had happened with Niall, to forget *him*.

The terracotta pots on her patio needed replanting for the summer, she reminded herself. She would call at the garden centre on the way home and buy some plants. That way at least she would keep physically busy.

She knew that she was right to force herself to go on with her life, to live it just as she had done before she had known Niall, but her heart wasn't really in what she was doing, she acknowledged later as she walked round the garden centre.

Everyone else seemed to be in couples or family groups, something she had never really noticed before. Only she seemed to be alone. And, even worse, instead of concentrating on choosing plants appropriate for her pots she found herself drawn to a display of herbs, set out in a traditional garden formation enclosed by small box hedges, something that would have been ideally suited to Niall's garden.

Hastily she redirected her footsteps to another part of the centre. That would be Beth's task to choose plants for their garden, not hers.

But when Niall had asked her for her help with

the house he had claimed that Beth wasn't interested in that kind of domestic detail. *Had* that been
true, or had it simply been a male ploy designed to
ensure *their* continued intimacy?

She shuddered suddenly, coming to a complete
standstill. Would he and Beth share the same bed
where he had made love to her? Her stomach
heaved at the thought, her skin suddenly damp with
perspiration. She felt sick with guilt and shame, unable to continue with the task that had originally
brought her to the garden centre.

She had behaved in a way that was totally and
completely out of character for her, but that did
nothing to lessen the weight of the burden she was
carrying.

As she stood in her sitting-room her glance was
caught by the photograph of her parents. She picked
it up and held it. What would her parents have
thought of her behaviour? Had she any need to ask
herself? They would have been shocked and dis-
tressed, hurt by her apparent rejection of the values
which had been so important to them; values she
had clung to as her only life raft after she had lost
them.

Her doorbell was ringing. Automatically she
went to answer it, still clutching the photograph.

No sixth sense warned her as she opened the
door, and the sight of Niall standing outside was so

unexpected and such a shock that she could only stand there, staring at him, as the photograph frame slipped from her fingers.

It was Niall who caught it. Niall who closed the door after he had walked into her hallway; Niall who demanded tersely, 'What is it? What's wrong? Are you ill?'

Ill? Slowly Lucy focused on him. Ill! Suddenly she wanted to scream the truth at him. Yes, she was ill. Sick with self-loathing, with guilt, with pain, sick with the knowledge of loving him; with having betrayed all the beliefs on which she had founded her life, but of course she could say none of these things because to do so would be to lose control, to give way to emotions she had no right to feel.

What was he doing here anyway? She had told him that she didn't want to see him again. The sale of the cottage was being dealt with by their respective solicitors. Had boredom, the lack of a sexual partner…the sexual loneliness of being without Beth brought him here to her?

Her gorge rose at the thought.

She turned her back on him, curling her fingers into her palms as she fought down the ache of longing rising up inside her, threatening to destroy her self-control and her resolve.

'Go away,' she told him harshly. 'I don't want you here.'

She could feel his tension even without looking at him.

'There's something we have to discuss,' she heard him saying grimly.

Her muscles tensed. Here it was…the moment she had been expecting ever since she had woken up in his bed and remembered Beth. He had come to ask her to keep what had happened between them to herself…to plead that he had never meant it to happen…to plead that Beth's peace of mind must be their first consideration. Her stomach twisted with an unbearable mixture of pain and love. Did he really think she was the kind of woman who would do that…who could cause hurt to another woman, an innocent woman? Why not? she derided herself. After all, she had scarcely taken Beth into consideration when she slept with him, had she?

'It's all right,' she told him bitterly, still not daring to risk looking at him. 'I know what you're going to say. I'm not going to tell anyone about what happened. Did you think I might really want to? Do you think it's something I'm proud of… something I *want* others to know about?'

She swung round then, protected by the fierce surge of the anger boiling inside her.

'Well, for your information, that's isn't how I feel. Letting anyone…anyone at all know what happened between us is the last thing *I* want.

'It's left me feeling too ashamed...too...too sick-
ened for that. I loathe myself because of it, and I
loathe you even more.'

The expression in his eyes wasn't one she had
ever encountered before. It made her heart hammer
in shocked fright as she recognised the ferocity of
his anger. He took a step towards her and then
stopped as she flinched.

'It's all right, Lucy,' he told her quietly, his voice
ice-cold. 'I wasn't going to inflict my loathsome
touch on you. As a matter of fact, what I *did* come
here for was to ensure that there hadn't been
any...repercussions—shall we say?—from our...
intimacy.'

He was asking her if she was pregnant, Lucy recognised. What would she have said if he had asked
her that question before she had gone to France?
Thank God he had not done so. Bitterness flooded
her. If she *had* been pregnant no doubt he would
have counselled her to have a termination, quietly
and discreetly, without causing anyone any embarrassment.

His relationship with Beth had to be protected at
all costs. And if *she* had to suffer, well, that was
her responsibility, wasn't it?

'No...there haven't been any repercussions,' she
told him stonily.

He was still holding her parents' photograph. He

put it down on the table, carefully adjusting the angle of it as though the small task were the most important thing he had to do, and then as he straightened he asked her quietly, 'Are you sure this is really what they would want for you, Lucy, a lonely, loveless, sterile life?'

It was more than she could bear. She could feel the emotions choking her as she told him shakily, 'What they would have wanted for me has nothing…nothing to do with you. Now will you please leave?'

After he had gone she put the safety chain across the door, although common sense told her that he was hardly likely to come back, never mind try to force an entry.

She stared round her sitting-room. The late-evening sunshine cast lozenges of warm gold light on the walls and the floor, but their warmth could not touch the icy cold misery filling her.

'YOU HAVEN'T forgotten that it's the first committee meeting for the fête tonight, have you?'

'No,' Lucy assured Verity.

'Good. I'll pick you up, shall I? About half-seven.'

Lucy grimaced to herself as she replaced the receiver. Attending the committee meeting was the last thing she felt like, but she acknowledged that it was something she would just have to do.

She was ready when Verity arrived to collect her at just gone seven-thirty. She had changed out of her office clothes and into a floral cotton skirt, over which she was wearing an oatmeal-coloured cotton-knit jumper.

In her bag she had a notepad and a couple of pens, since she suspected that it would probably fall to her to act as secretary and to take notes of what she suspected initially would be an extremely con-fused and unproductive meeting. No doubt even-tually calm would be created out of chaos and the fête would be as it always was, a minor success, raising a modest sum of money, and causing every-one involved with it to bask in a self-righteous glow of having done their bit for the local community.

What was the matter with her? Lucy asked her-self miserably as she followed Verity out to her car. She never used to be so cynical...so critical.

But then she knew, didn't she, what lay at the root of her malaise, that her feelings were a direct consequence, an overspill in effect, of all the self-contempt and the loathing she felt for herself.

'Don told me about Niall buying the cottage. You must be very relieved,' Verity commented as she drove.

'Yes,' Lucy agreed hollowly.

'It's the ideal solution, really, isn't it?' Verity persisted. Lucy nodded, thankful to see the church hall come into view. The last thing she wanted was to discuss Niall with Verity or with anyone else. Just hearing someone else say his name was enough to break through the defences she had tried to erect against everything she felt for him. Just thinking about him was enough to make her heart ache with longing and with pain.

'We're here,' Verity announced unnecessarily, parking her car with more verve than skill.

There were several other cars parked outside the hall. Lucy gave them an uninterested look as she and Verity walked across the car park.

'Looks as if almost everyone else has arrived,' Verity commented as they reached the hall.

The committee was of necessity a rather large and unwieldy one. There were so many local interests that wanted to be represented at the fête, and offence could so easily be caused by excluding any one of them.

The arguments they would have this evening in trying to sort out some kind of agenda for the event were nothing to those which would come later when rivalling factions fought over who had the best claim to the most advantageous sites and stalls, as Lucy knew from experience.

Several tables had been pushed together with

chairs placed around them. The vicar was there, looking slightly harassed and rather tired. Lucy smiled automatically, returning the 'hello's of the others.

This year it was Verity's turn to be chairperson, and now, as she called everyone to order and to their seats, she started counting heads, commenting, 'I think almost everyone's here now, aren't they? We've got a new committee member this year, and one who I think will be a great asset to us. Ah, here he is now.'

Lucy turned round automatically as the hall door opened, her body paralysed with shock as Niall walked in.

'Niall, come and sit down here next to Lucy,' Verity commanded. 'She'll show you the ropes.

'Niall—Mr Cameron—has offered to sponsor some of our competition events,' Verity announced, smiling warmly at Niall as he walked towards the assembled group.

There were several empty chairs, but, as Verity had suggested, he took the one next to Lucy's, pulling it out and sitting down.

Even though she had not properly looked at him, she was acutely conscious of him. He had brought into the room with him the smell of fresh air, but more than that Lucy was aware of the subtle personal male scent of him, her body so closely attuned to it that already her heart was pounding, her muscles tensing against the weakening wave of love that swept over her, demolishing her defences.

Verity was introducing Niall to the rest of the committee. Lucy kept her head bent over her note-book, refusing to look at him, praying for the meeting to be over.

If she had known that Niall was to be one of its members there was no way she would ever have agreed to be on the committee.

All around her people were talking, busily trying to get across the claims of their particular group, while Verity tried to get some kind of order into the conflicting suggestions and appeals being made.

The first meeting of the year was always like this. Lucy made brief notes, glad of something to occupy her, to prevent her from having to acknowledge Niall's presence at her side.

So far he had not said anything, but she could feel his alertness, his interest in everything that was going on. She knew that it was an act of genuine generosity for him to volunteer to sponsor some of their competitive events. Without such sponsors the fête would not even get off the ground, but she was still consumed with bitter misery as she fought against the mental image tormenting her—Niall dressed in cool summer clothes, Beth clinging lovingly to his arm in some filmy feminine outfit, smil-

ing prettily as they presented the prizes...an acknowledged, accepted couple, while she stood on
the sidelines...excluded...unwanted.

At eight-thirty they broke for coffee. Lucy sat,
silently wrapped in a numbing cloak of misery, as
she listened to the chatter going on all around her.

Verity leaned across her and said archly to Niall,
'Still no news of when Beth is due back? You must
miss her dreadfully. I know I hate it when Don has
to go away even for a few days.'

'I do miss her,' Niall agreed. 'But she has her
own life to lead, and, after all, it isn't as though
we're a married couple.'

'Oh, no, of course not,' Verity agreed hastily.
'Although these days...well, marriage is just one
option, and when two people are in love with one
another...'

'I think there seems to have been some sort of
misunderstanding about the nature of my relationship with Beth,' Niall announced drily after giving
Verity a very alert, sharply thoughtful glance. 'Beth
is my sister, not my lover.'

Lucy felt the room start to spin dizzily round her.
Oh, no, please not again, she prayed as she felt her
hold on full consciousness slipping...racing dangerously away from her.

She could hear Verity's voice, but couldn't make
out exactly what she was saying. She tried to push

back her chair, to excuse herself, to escape before it was too late, but her muscles seemed to have turned to lead, her body heavy, her movements slow.

WHEN SHE CAME round she was outside, sitting on an old wooden bench beside the hall, and Niall was sitting next to her, his hand gently holding the nape of her neck.

As she lifted her head from where it was resting on her knees she heard him asking her, 'Are you all right?'

She nodded. Fainting...again. What a stupid... stupid thing to do.

She flushed hotly as she realised that everyone else inside the hall must have seen her faint, must be wondering...

'It's OK,' Niall told her as though he had known her thoughts. 'Verity said she'd explain to everyone that you hadn't been feeling very well. A small touch of food poisoning.'

Food poisoning! Lucy licked her dry lips and gave him a wild, confused glance.

'Why *did* you faint, Lucy?'

She turned her head away; her body was wet with perspiration, her heart was beating far, far too fast. If she had been physically capable of doing so she would have got up and run, not walked, away from him.

'Look at me, Lucy,' he commanded.

She didn't. She couldn't.

'I fainted because...because it was so warm in the hall,' she lied, gabbling the words, knowing that they wouldn't even begin to deceive him but unable to think of anything else.

Silence.

She ached to turn her head and to see what he was thinking, but she dared not.

'I see. So you didn't faint, then, because you'd just realised that Beth was my sister and not my lover.'

It was worse, far worse than she had dreaded. She knew he must have guessed, of course, but she had hoped, prayed, that he wouldn't say so; that he wouldn't strip her completely bare of her defences and challenge her like this.

She couldn't help it. Emotion choked her, far too strong for her to suppress. A tear glistened at the corner of one eye.

'I'm sorry,' she told him brokenly. 'I'm so sorry.'

She was past hiding anything from him now, too shocked to make any attempt to conceal what she was feeling.

'And so you should be. How *could* you think that?'

She could hear his anger and she couldn't blame him for it. She bit down hard on her bottom lip, willing her tears not to fall, but her body shook with the force of her pain.

'Oh, Lucy, Lucy, how *could* you have believed that there was anyone else?' he demanded, but his voice was different now, rough with an emotion that wasn't anger.

She felt him take hold of her and turn her round to face him. Her face was flushed, her eyes wet with tears. She looked a complete mess, she thought fretfully; no female over fourteen could cry and not do so.

'How could there *possibly* be anyone else after the way we loved one another?'

It was more than she could stand.

If he had been angry with her, contemptuous of her, bitter, she could have withstood it better, but this...this patent anguish and pain...

Her control deserted her completely and she wept heartbrokenly, trying to cover her face with her hands, but Niall wouldn't let her.

'I love you,' he told her softly. 'Surely you must have known that...must have seen...have felt...? Or was it just that it was easier, safer to pretend that there was a moral and physical barrier between us than to admit that you were afraid to love me in return?'

'No,' Lucy protested, shocked out of her distress by his words. She looked at him, frowning, as she repeated huskily, 'No…I…I was afraid…yes, but when we…when you…when you touched me somehow I forgot my fear; somehow it no longer seemed important, valid.' Her own confusion that she should have felt like that showed in her voice.

'Poor Lucy,' Niall said gently. 'It *was* all a bit too much for you, wasn't it? There you were, hugging your self-control against you like a security blanket, swearing that you weren't going to love anyone, and then suddenly you discovered that there are some things in life over which we have no control, about which we have no real choice. You must have been very frightened.'

'Terrified,' Lucy admitted.

It hurt her that he was showing such a clear understanding of her, and it hurt her because she had had no similar understanding of him. *Was* he right? Had a small part of her wanted to believe that he was committed to someone else because she had been afraid?

'It was after I lost my parents,' she told him unsteadily. 'I felt so afraid, so alone. All my life they had been there, loving me, protecting me, and then suddenly they weren't. It was such a horrible feeling…'

She shuddered, her eyes blank as she relived those months after her parents' death.

'Perhaps I was too sensitive...too vulnerable. I was an only child...I *enjoyed* being with my parents. We did a lot of things together. I had friends, but...perhaps I was too close to them, I don't know.'

'You loved them, and when you lost them it hurt so much that you told yourself you must never risk that kind of pain again, is that it?' Niall asked her.

Lucy nodded.

'How...how did you know?'

'I know because I know everything there is to know about you, Lucy. I've made an intensive study of you. Initially, I admit, it was because of the situation with Eric. I was confused then; all the things I was learning about you seemed so directly opposed to the picture Eric had drawn of you, and then I met you. People...all people carry their own auras around with them, the unseen shadows, if you like, of their own personalities, and yours was so obviously that of a person who, although very well liked and with very good friends, rejected any kind of real intimacy, and that intrigued me because it was plain that you weren't cold; that you weren't a loner by nature, but by choice, and I wanted to know why you had made that choice. By the time I found out I had been forced to acknowledge that my interest was no longer merely academic, that in fact you had become something of an obsession with me; that I wanted...no, *needed* desperately to break through that barrier you'd grown around yourself...that I needed desperately to reach out to you and to have you reach out to me.

'I thought of trying all the conventional methods, but I suspected you simply would not want to know. You made it so clear that you weren't interested...that you didn't want me in your life, but when I touched you...well, then it was different. Then the messages your body gave mine said that you *weren't* indifferent to me at all, and by then I knew enough about you to know that you were the kind of woman who could only respond so immediately to a man to whom you were emotionally as well as physically responsive. So in desperation I decided to take a calculated risk.

'If I could only make you give yourself to me totally physically I thought it would enable me to reach out to you emotionally. I thought it had worked, as well...

'Until I woke up and found that you'd left me. Until you told me that you wanted nothing more to do with me. Until you told me that you had found my touch loathsome.'

He felt the shudder that went through her.

'Lucy, Lucy...I love you *so much*. Why *didn't*

you talk to me about Beth? Why didn't you tell me?'

She shook her head, unable to speak.

Her throat felt raw, but she forced herself to speak, her voice croaky and filled with pain.

'I felt so ashamed,' she told him. 'I knew, because Verity had told me even before I met you, that you were living with someone…that you were committed to her, and yet I still couldn't control the way I felt about you. I made love with you, knowing that I had no right to do so, and I hated myself for that. You see, I've always believed that loving someone, wanting someone, is no excuse for self-indulgently taking what you want, when there is someone else involved, someone else who will be hurt, and to discover that I could not control my feelings…' She broke off, shivering, as Niall drew her closer against his body.

'And then when you said that Beth had nothing to do with us I thought you were telling me that all it had been was sex. I told myself it was what I deserved, but it didn't help. It didn't stop me loving you.'

'So you do love me, then?'

She looked at him.

'Oh, Niall,' she said shakily.

He was smiling at her, the kind of smile that

made her toes curl and a slow, strong surge of warmth permeate her whole body.

'Was that a yes?' he teased her softly.

She smiled then, her lips parting on a sudden surge of breathless excitement as she saw the way he was looking at her.

'Not here,' he told her, but his hand still cupped her jaw, his fingers stroking her face with the tenderness she had remembered so vividly and so tormentingly in her lonely misery.

'Come on,' he said softly. 'Let's go home.'

Arm in arm, they walked over to the Discovery, but it wasn't until he turned into the drive that she realised that by 'home' he had meant her flat.

The moment they were inside he took her in his arms.

Against her mouth he said fiercely, 'Don't ever, *ever* doubt my love for you again, Lucy, and please don't reject me either. I don't think I could stand it.'

And then he was kissing her with a hunger that made her heart turn over and her body go weak.

She responded to him with feverish eagerness, desperate to show him how much she cared, how much she regretted her own inability to recognise the honesty of his love.

As he released her Niall asked her, 'Shall we tell them now?'

And when she looked at him in confusion he went on, 'Your parents, Lucy. Shall we tell them now that you aren't going to be alone any longer; that you aren't afraid of love any more; that you aren't denying all that they gave you by being afraid to love?'

As they walked into the sitting-room and he picked up her parents' photograph he told her somberly, 'We never lose the love people give us, Lucy. It's always there...always a part of our lives.'

He was right, she recognised.

Tears filled her eyes, but this time they were tears of joy and not tears of pain.

'I love you, Niall Cameron,' she told him shakily.

SIX WEEKS LATER she was saying the same words to him as they stood together in front of the altar, exchanging their marriage vows.

Beth had flown back from New York for the wedding, no longer plump-faced and girlish-looking, as she had been in her photograph, but a sleekly sophisticated young woman who was openly amused to learn that Lucy had at one time totally misjudged her relationship with her brother.

'Are you sure you really don't mind Eric living with us while the cottage is repaired?' Niall asked her during the reception.

Lovingly Lucy shook her head, leaning over to kiss him.

'Eric and I have made our peace,' she assured him, and it was true. 'And, besides, it's only for a couple of months, and he *is* your uncle, after all.'

'Yours too now,' Niall reminded her. 'Not exactly a romantically appealing Cupid...'

'But very effective, none the less,' Lucy countered.

'Very effective,' Niall agreed, returning her kiss.

'Hey, you two, save that for the honeymoon,' Beth admonished them, laughing.

'Mm...the honeymoon. Now that's something I am looking forward to,' Niall whispered in Lucy's ear. 'How about you?'

'I could be,' Lucy temporised, and then laughed as she saw the look in his eyes and admitted, 'I can hardly wait. Just the two of us. On our own.' Her eyes showed what she was feeling. Niall's hand tensed on her arm.

'Just the two of us,' he promised. 'And the rest of our lives together.'

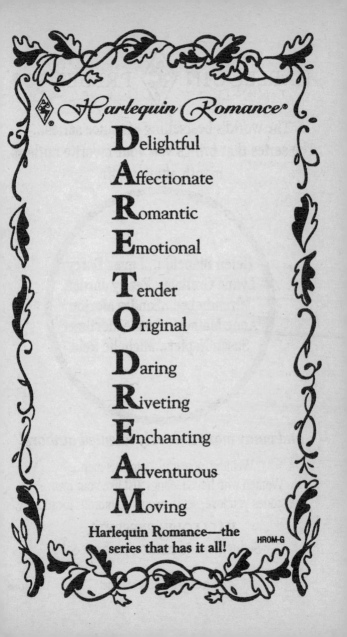

Harlequin Romance®

Delightful

Affectionate

Romantic

Emotional

Tender

Original

Daring

Riveting

Enchanting

Adventurous

Moving

Harlequin Romance—the
series that has it all!

HROM-G

Harlequin® Historical

From rugged lawmen and
valiant knights to defiant heiresses
and spirited frontierswomen,
Harlequin Historicals will
capture your imagination with
their dramatic scope, passion
and adventure.

Harlequin Historicals...
they're too good to miss!

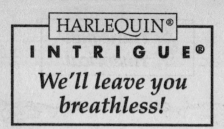

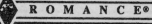

Makes any time special.™

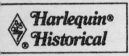